SEARCH A DARKER SKY

A
CLEFT
MIND

DEVIK SCHREINER

Search a Darker Sky. A Cleft Mind.

© 2011 Devik Schreiner

ISBN: 978-1-61170-038-1

Cover art and illustrations by Jeanne Marie Yee.

Printed in the USA and UK on acid free paper.

For additional copies of this book go to:
www.rp–author.com/dschreiner

 **Robertson Publishing**
59 N. Santa Cruz Avenue, Suite B.
Los Gatos, California 95030 USA
www.RobertsonPublishing.com

To every kid who had a reason to quit
but never did.

Acknowledgements

To my wife, Susanna, for always believing in me. To Sarah Jo Smith, for her optimism, spot-on analysis and detailed feedback. To Jeanne Marie Yee, for her inspiring artwork, and for keeping the fire lit under my rear end. To the editing team of Marcia Wolf and Yonatan Margalit, for their insightful comments and crucial opinions. To Justin Jones and Cooper Wilson, for using their heads. To my mother, Manuela, who kept me fascinated when I was a little boy by reading me stories and giving characters different voices. To my amazing sister, Geoffa, who always has my back. And finally, to all my students over the years, for their energy, critical honesty, and excitement.

Preface

It's been dark a long time. I've been on the road, I don't know how long, going somewhere. The seat next to mine is empty. My reflection stares back at me from the big black window. I keep thinking it has to be morning soon.

Mrs. Hooper, you had this journal, with the strange phrase on the cover, "A Cleft Mind," for three years, before you gave it to me. It's weird using it to write to you, my teacher. I've only known you for a few days, but there's a lot you never told me while you had the chance.

You made me promise I'd write in it every day, and I told you I would. Too much happened those first few days to keep that promise. But now, here I am, with nothing but time. Time, and a small box I haven't opened. And a news article about a sick kid. And a napkin with a cop's name on it. And the journal. My whole life is in a plastic shopping bag.

I'm so sick of buses.

CHAPTER 1:
The Journal

It was the first day of sixth grade, the last year of elementary school. You wrote on the white board in big capital letters:

WHO AM I? WHO ARE YOU?

We sat silently, waiting for you to speak. You didn't. You just looked at us. We looked back at you. It was quiet. It went on too long. Everyone seemed uncomfortable, except you. Did you look at me longer than at the other kids, or was that my imagination?

Finally, you spoke. We breathed. You gave us the standard introduction, telling us about yourself, your husband, the reasons you became a teacher. Then you asked us to write about ourselves for ten minutes, and finish it for homework. You have my original, but I'll write as much as I can remember of it here, in the journal:

Name: Justin Tyme

Age: 11.5

One morning, about three years ago, I said goodbye to my dad, and my mom drove me to school. Like what happened every morning for as long as I can remember, except for one thing: I never saw my dad again.

I've asked my mom what happened. She says she doesn't want to talk about it. If she says anything at all. I think she's depressed. I worry about her.

I have friends whose mom and dad have divorced. They told me that there was a lot of arguing during their parents' separation. My parents didn't argue at all. I know I was only 8 at the time, but I would have remembered them yelling at each other. Besides, my dad wouldn't just leave. He loved my mom, me, and my little sister, Alyssa, a lot. And he loved his job as an architect.

My step-dad's name is Frank Summers. He's been with my mom since my dad disappeared, almost to the day. I think it's weird that my mom would move on to another guy so quickly. Especially a man so completely different than my dad.

Frank is big and intimidating. He's tall, bald, and his body is shaped like a giant barbell. With all the muscle in his neck and shoulders, I don't know how he can even move his head. Every morning, he stands in front of the bathroom mirror, lathers up his scalp with shaving cream, and drags a razor across it, slowly, row by row, back to front, like he's mowing a little lawn on top of his head.

There's a tattoo on his right arm. I don't think he knows that I know. I had never seen him without a long-sleeved shirt on, even on hot days. But about three months ago, when I came home from school, he was napping on the couch, wearing a tank top, and I saw it.

The tat is big. It covers most of his bulging biceps and triceps. It's oval-shaped with a black border, and has a yellow patch in the middle. Inside the patch, there are four black pillars connected by an arch. On each pillar is a downward-facing green dagger. Along the arch, there are four green stars. Four words are inked in the yellow patch: "Smarter, Faster, Stronger, Better." The number '94' is on the left side, and a capital "B" is on the right. There are some smaller letters too, but I couldn't read them.

Across the entire tattoo, there's a silhouette of a fox. Or at least, I think it's a fox. It's so light that it's almost a shadow. The whole thing looks like it would have taken a long time to do. And would have hurt.

I guess it's weird that I know the tattoo in such detail. It's just that I know so little about him. I thought that the tattoo might have some meaning.

Frank is less loving than my dad. Less interested in my sister and me. OK, that's not true. He's not loving, and not interested in us at all. But he does provide for us, something he reminds us of all the time. We have food, and clothes, and a roof over our heads.

One thing he does care about is his work. He's very involved with it. When he's not home, he's at work. Except I don't know where that is. Or what it is. I asked him once what he did. He told me, "I work in the world of money." That doesn't really narrow it down, since pretty much all jobs have to do with money. And he said it like he wasn't taking any more questions.

Those short answers are typical. If what he says to me doesn't have to do with keeping the house neat, clean, and organized, then he doesn't talk to me, period. Most of the time, he acts as though Alyssa and I don't even exist. Sometimes, when we're doing our homework on the living room floor, he'll step right over us, like we're puddles on the street and he's trying to keep from getting his shoes wet.

About a year ago, my mom had my little brother, Frank, Jr. He's really cute. He's got chunky cheeks and these wide, puppy-dog eyes. He's a really fast crawler, and last week he stood up for a couple of seconds. I think walking is right around the corner. The silly faces he makes really crack me and Alyssa up. And the way he smears food on his face is hilarious.

You'd think that a father would show a little affection toward his own baby. But I've never seen Frank even pick him up, or pay any attention to him at all. His own son and he ignores him. And ignores my mom, too.

(End of "WHO AM I?" assignment)

3

Fast-forward to lunchtime. I was sitting with my best friend Mike at one of the picnic tables and you walked over to us.

"Justin, do you have a few minutes you could spare?" you asked. "I'd like a word with you in my classroom."

Mike gave me a look like he was asking, "What's this about?" Before I had a chance to even shrug, I was sitting at a desk in the front row of your room, squirming in my seat.

Being the only kid in the classroom can be bad. But, since it was the first day of school, what could I have already done? The door closed behind me, and the hysteria of playground screams morphed into the hum of the air conditioner. You sat at the desk next to mine. My "WHO AM I?" assignment was in your hands.

I imagined what I would hear next:

Justin, I've reviewed your assignment. Based on your writing ability, I'm concerned that sixth grade is going to be too challenging for you. How would you feel about joining your friends in the fifth grade again this year? It would give you a great opportunity to work on your skills…

Or maybe you'd say…

Justin, I read your paper. It sounds like your home life is a real challenge for you. You need a chance to process your feelings. I'd like to enroll you in counseling twice a week, at least to start. Then, each week, you'll go one additional day, including Saturdays…

You cleared your throat. "Justin, I read your assignment. I think you're a very talented writer. Do you enjoy writing?"

You caught me off guard— I wasn't prepared for a compliment. And then, my mind went blank. It was as if I accidentally pushed the 'delete' button in my brain and erased all of my thoughts. I knew I had to say something, but I couldn't. You had mercy on me and gave me another chance.

"Justin, do you like to write?"

"I, yeah, I guess. I guess so."

Wow, brilliant response. Very impressive. For a second I wished I could turn myself into a gopher and disappear into a hole that would open up in the floor. But I was still there.

I never thought about it before you asked me. I always liked assignments that involved writing, but not because I actually *enjoyed* them; they just seemed easier than my other homework.

But I did like writing to you about my family situation. After I finished the "Who Am I?" assignment, I felt like some weight had been lifted off my shoulders. Maybe it was because, for the first time, someone else knew a little about how things were for me at home.

"Justin," you asked, "would you like to do some extra credit for me this year?"

"I'm not sure," I said. "What would I have to do?"

"You'd keep a journal," you said. "You can write anything you want in it: stuff that happens to you, current events, feelings—anything you'd like. However, there is one important rule."

"What's that?"

"The rule is that you must write in your journal *every day*, without exception. Even when you're sick, or tired, or get home late. Even when you have absolutely nothing to write, you *have* to write. No excuses."

I imagined nighttime at the house, my step-dad marching down the hallway at exactly 8:30 and barking "Lights out!" If I accepted your extra credit assignment, it would mean doing a lot of writing under the covers, by flashlight. Frank would never tolerate his sleep command being disobeyed.

Only to Alyssa and a couple of friends did I use the nickname I have for him: "The Tank." Sis and I shared a room in the house that Frank bought right after he met my mom, and we were always on the lookout for his military patrols. He would enter a room determined to find something wrong, something me or Sis had moved or messed up. He really *was* like a tank, rolling through the house like he was conquering enemy territory in some great battle.

And even though there were two extra rooms in the house, the Tank refused to let me have one of them. He insisted that they be kept neat and almost empty for something he called "future use projects." One of the rooms was stacked with boxes.

But back to the extra credit. You explained to me that writing in the journal meant that if I missed a couple of assignments, it wouldn't hurt my grade as much. It also meant making a commitment to you. But that didn't sound too tough.

"OK, I'll do it," I said. "But what should I write in?"

"I have something for you," you said.

You walked over to a file cabinet behind your desk, slid open the bottom drawer, and pulled out what looked like an old scrapbook.

I had never seen anything like it. The cover was a faded leather-brown. Along the edges, a gold border reflected the fluorescent lights of the classroom. On the cover, there were inlaid black capital letters that spelled out **'A CLEFT MIND'**. I opened it to the first page. It was blank, yellowed with age, and rough to the touch. Then the bell rang.

"So, what do you think?" you asked me.

"What does 'A CLEFT MIND' mean?"

"I'm not sure," you said. "A couple years back, a friend of mine gave me this journal and told me to pass it on. I was waiting for the right person."

And what makes me the right person? I wondered. But I didn't ask. Looking back, maybe I should have.

"Put the journal in your backpack, take it home, and hide it somewhere safe. Bring it to school if you have to, but always keep a close eye on it." You looked toward the door and seemed nervous. Scared even.

"Now, if you'll excuse me, I need to prepare for class," you said. "Thanks for your time."

I slid the journal into my backpack, carefully avoiding scraping the journal's delicate edges against the zipper. My backpack felt five pounds heavier with the big book inside. I was walking toward the door when I heard your voice.

"Justin."

"Yeah?" I turned around.

"Don't forget."

"Don't forget what?"

"Write."

I didn't forget. I had every intention of writing. That night, after Frank ordered "Lights out!" and I was sure Alyssa, in the bed next to mine, was sleeping, I pulled the journal from my backpack and took it under my covers. I created a little tent by propping myself up on my elbows so my head held the covers away from the book, and balanced my flashlight on my pillow. It had to be angled just right to light up a page.

I opened the journal and ran my fingers over the thick, rough paper. I knew what I was going write about: my dad. All about him. Everything he ever did or said. All I could remember about him.

But as I lay there with my pen poised above the paper, I couldn't start. At that moment, I realized that writing the history of my father put him in the past tense. And I wasn't ready to do that. I wasn't ready to tell the story. It hadn't ended.

I had too many questions about why he was gone. And the only person who might have the answers, my mom, wouldn't talk to me.

That night, I didn't write a word. But I knew I would. Soon.

I heard the pounding of footsteps from one of the Tank's late night house patrols, clicked the flashlight off, and froze until the footsteps faded away. I closed the journal and slid it under my mattress. There was no way that Alyssa would find it there. My mom might have discovered it, when my dad was still with us. But she didn't even come into our room anymore. Maybe she just stopped caring.

The Tank was different. When I wasn't home, he trespassed. He went through my desk, the closet, even my dresser drawers. I didn't know what he was looking for. He left blue sticky notes with messages written in perfect capital letters:

A SHIRT FELL OUT OF YOUR HAMPER.
I PUT IT BACK. KEEP YOUR HAMPER
ORDERLY AT ALL TIMES.

Or:

I FOUND PAPER SHAVINGS
AND BITS OF ERASER IN YOUR
UPPER RIGHT-HAND DESK
DRAWER. KEEP YOUR DESK CLEAN.

When I got home from school and saw a sticky note, I got a sick feeling in the pit of my stomach. I didn't like to read them. I didn't like him going into our room. I wish I had the guts to tell him not to.

The Tank liked to tell Alyssa and me that we were only "renting" a room in the house — that our room belonged to *him*, and if we were going to live under *his* roof then we needed to follow *his* rules. But even renters have rights, don't they?

CHAPTER 2:
The Voice

My life was pretty much the same thing every day, and the morning after I brought home the journal was no exception. At exactly 6:30, the Tank crept into our room like he was on some secret mission, and silently snuck up to my bed. Slowly, he gripped the top of the covers and WHAM!— he ripped the covers off me, leaving me shocked and shivering. Not wanting to give him the satisfaction of startling me, I pretended to sleep through it.

Then the Tank yelled in his most obnoxious military voice, "UP AND ADAM, TYME! CHOW IN TEN MINUTES! BE THERE!" My mom used to wake us up. She was much more gentle.

I dragged myself down the hall for breakfast. Frank, Jr. was already in his high chair, smearing oatmeal on his face and every once in a while getting some into his mouth. Junior dropped his sippy cup on the floor and looked around to see if anyone noticed. Then he blurted out his favorite (and only) word: "UH-OH!" I picked up the cup and gave it back to him, telling him that he shouldn't throw it. He flashed me a gummy smile and giggled, and did it again.

Then, like clockwork, he pointed a fist towards the small TV on the kitchen counter and made these funny monkey noises while he slammed his little body against the back of his high chair.

That was his way of telling us that his show was on. I was

sick of it, but I tolerated it because I knew it gave Mom time to have her coffee and a cigarette out back. I got up from the table and turned on the TV.

And there was the voice, half circus announcer, half crazed maniac:

"LADIES AND GENTLEMEN, BOYS AND GIRLS, ALIENS AND EARTHLINGS! IT'S TIME FOR EVERYBODY'S FAVORITE HALF-HOUR OF TELEVISION! BUCKLE YOUR SEAT BELTS, STOW AWAY YOUR TRAY TABLES, PUT YOUR BRAINS IN THE UPRIGHT POSITION, AND GET READY TO CRASH LAND WITH THE MOST LOVABLE GROUP OF GEOMETRIC FIGURES THE UNIVERSE HAS EVER KNOWN! IT'S... RONNY RECTAN-GLE AND THE SUPER-SHAPES!" (WILD APPLAUSE)

Ronny Rectangle is this goofy cartoon character, a big, green, fuzzy geometric shape with a bright red smiley face where his stomach should be. Instead of arms and legs, Ronny has different tools attached to him: ruler, protractor, compass, and calculator. During each episode he encounters different challenges, and he uses his tools to meet them.

He doesn't do it alone. The Super-Shapes are Ronny's help-ers. There's Sally Circle, sensitive and shy, always holding a piece of pie with the number 3.14 on it. Tony Triangle is sharp-minded, always trying to make a point. Polly-Gone is multi-faceted and moody, running away at the first sign of trouble.

The Super-Shapes sing corny songs with positive messages for their young audience. There's "Inch Your Way Along," "Try a Different Angle," and "You'll Always Measure Up." The dia-logue is way too advanced for Junior to follow, but Mom told me that it's good for his brain. That is, when she used to talk to me.

And Junior did seem to be trying hard to understand what was going on with Ronny and the gang. When he recognized a song, he turned to Alyssa and me and pointed a fist toward the TV like he was saying, "Hey, I know that one!"

It was time to go to school. Mom had stopped driving me to school soon after we moved in with the Tank, three years ago. As Lissy and I were leaving the house for the bus stop, I yelled, "Bye, Mom!" There was no response from her, no "Have a good day!" or "I love you, kids!" It didn't surprise me, but still, it was sad, because I think my sister thought it was normal. It had gone on since she was four-years-old.

The bus stop was a couple of blocks from the house. I was walking, kind of spacing out, when I realized that my sister was talking to me. I think it was about school, or something she saw on TV. Then she paused for a minute and looked up at me with big, innocent eyes, peeking out from behind long bangs. Squinting against the early morning sun, she flicked a lock of hair from her face.

"Justin, where's daddy?"

She asked me almost every day since he'd been gone. And every day, I told her the truth.

"I don't know, Sis."

The bus rolled up. We got on and she sat in the seat across from the driver, next to her best friend, Julie. Seemed like the older you got, the farther back you sat. I saw my buddy Mike and headed back toward him.

I had known Mike Brainerd since first grade. Even back then, he was the smartest kid in the class. While the other kids were at recess, jumping rope or playing handball, Mike was inside working on something called "Definitive Parabolic Equations." While we finger-painted stick figures during art, Mike was memorizing Pi to one hundred places. In fourth grade, he took the SATs and scored a perfect 1600. There was even an article about him in the newspaper.

In fifth grade, Mike worked on what he called his ABC's—Advanced Bachelor's Curriculum. He was doing college work in the classroom while the other kids were learning regular fifth grade stuff. Every Monday, a tutor came to school and met with Mike, assigning him his work for the week.

I asked him once why his parents, who were both doctors, didn't put him in a school for gifted kids. He told me that they thought it was important for him to be in a normal, public school environment. And, despite his intelligence, Mike was a pretty down-to-earth guy. He was nice to be around and didn't act like he was better than anyone.

But some of the boys at school gave him a hard time. They called him "Brain," a nickname he pretended not to mind, and teased him using a voice they made sound like a robot:

"HELLO BRAIN, DO YOU COMPUTE? WILL YOU DO MY HOMEWORK FOR ME?"

"Hey, Justin, what's happening?" he asked.

I appreciated when Mike spoke at my level. Although he didn't mean to, he had a tendency to use vocabulary that only a college professor could understand. He scooted over to the window seat and I sat down next to him, gently laying my backpack on the floor so the journal wouldn't get smashed. We rode in silence.

My dad once told me: "A true friend is someone with whom there's no such thing as an uncomfortable silence." If my dad was right, Mike was a true friend. We looked out the window and drove past a park.

My mom and dad used to take us to the park a lot. While

Alyssa played in the sand, my dad timed me running through an obstacle course that we set up: Up the stairs, down the slide, around the swings, through the merry-go-round, back up the stairs, and down the slide again.

The tough part was that each time I ran past him, he asked me a question: "Six times nine!" or "Second President of the United States!" — "Spell 'broccoli'!" For each incorrect answer, he added five seconds to my time. Sometimes Sis wanted to play, so for her he asked easy questions while she ran around, but most of the time she laughed so hard that she had to stop.

My dad also used to say, "When it's time to play, we play. When it's time to work, we work." That meant homework. Alyssa and I sat at the kitchen table. I worked on my assignments while my dad read and my sister drew with crayons. My mom would either hang out with us or would go for a walk with a friend of hers.

With both my parents around, I knew that if I needed help with schoolwork, someone was there for me. I could never ask the Tank for help. Somehow, without even saying it, he made it perfectly clear that he had no time for me and Alyssa.

My mom and dad used to talk and laugh a lot. I never really paid attention to their conversations; I just remember the warm, comforting murmur of their voices. At the Tank's house, there was no talking and laughing. Except for the TV, it might as well have been a library. Quiet. Still. Sterile. There weren't even any pictures on the walls.

My dad's disappearance wasn't the result of a separation. It was different than that. I felt it in my gut. Something happened. I didn't know what, but my mom knew. She had to. And I had tried to talk to her about it, more times than I could count. I always waited until I was alone with her, in case she didn't want to talk in front of the Tank.

"Mom, you got a minute?" I would ask.

"What is it, Justin?" She knew what was coming next. The questions would just fall out of me.

"What happened between you and dad? Why did he leave all of a sudden? Where is he?"

"Justin." She would have this blank look on her face.

"What?"

"You know I don't like talking about that."

"Why not?" I would press her.

"Justin, I just don't want to talk about it. Can't you respect that?"

The conversation to nowhere. Always dead before it started.

Can't you respect that?

No Mom, I can't, not anymore.

Finding out what happened to my dad was the most important thing in my life. I was going to do it with or without my mom's help.

CHAPTER 3:
The Toe Birds

Our bus was always the first to arrive at school. I stepped off, pulled on my backpack, and watched Mike, Lissy and Julie walk up the path toward the office and disappear into the library.

There was something new, something fresh, about a cold, clear school day. The smell of fresh-cut grass. The dew-covered field, still un-invaded by a thousand footprints. The four tall palm trees that cast their long, clean shadows.

I went up the main path, past the office, and made a left around the corner. To my right were the first and second grade classrooms. Past the back entrance to the library, there was a blue door with the word "JANITOR" painted in clumsy white letters. I looked around, making sure no one was looking. Kids from the early buses were supposed to go straight to the library.

I knocked three times. Footsteps from the inside grew louder. Two knocks came back at me. I gave one solid knock back.

"Come in, little buddy. It's open."

The voice was low-pitched and gravely. I took one last look behind me. Just pigeons pecking some invisible crumbs. I pulled on the door and stepped inside.

The smell was the first thing that hit me. The fresh morning air was gone, replaced by a mixture of bleach, motor oil, and coffee. It was a weird combination, but my nose quickly got used to it.

A dim, spiderweb-covered light bulb lit up a long hallway. The lyrics to a rock song I had heard a hundred times echoed to-ward me:

> *Get on that Hog my friend,*
> *Our good times will never end,*
> *As long as we have half a tank of gas,*
> *We'll burn rubber while they kiss our —*

Posters hung crookedly on the hallway walls. Harley-David-sons, painted black with red flames. Smoke billowing from the exhaust pipes of muscle cars. Growling dragsters waiting for the green light. There was a door at the end of the hall. It creaked open.

A man with long, frizzy black hair was sitting at a desk, his back to me, drumming to the beat of the song. The desk was piled so high with magazines, motorcycle parts, and containers of old food that at any second I expected to see the whole mountain come crashing down.

The man spun around in his chair. He had on dirty jeans and a yellow smiley-face T-shirt, with a well-worn black leather vest over it. His friendly face was covered with a scruffy, black beard and mustache.

"Hey, what's going on, Justin? Wanna donut?" He pushed an open box toward me and I took one.

Mr. Dave had been at Ben Harrison Elementary for twenty-four years, and for the last two, I had visited him in his office al-most every morning. It actually started a year before that, when I won a contest at school called "In Their Shoes." School employ-ees pulled tickets with students' names on them, lottery style, and Mr. Dave pulled my name. The next day, I got to spend a few hours with him, learning about his responsibilities at school. He called it "shadowing."

I liked shadowing Mr. Dave, but most of all, I enjoyed talking to him. He laughed a lot and made jokes. At the end of the day, he invited me to visit him in his office if I ever had the time. I found the time in the mornings.

Mr. Dave drove a hog (slang for a Harley-Davidson) that he parked in the last space in the far end of the parking lot. When the bus pulled up to school in the morning, it was good to see the hog; I knew he was already there.

But the morning after I got the journal, I felt uncomfortable. I was going to talk to Mr. Dave about my dad. It was going to be the first time I had talked to anyone about him, not counting my mom and Sis.

"Can I ask you something?" I said.

"Wasn't that something already?" he said with a wicked smile. Mr. Dave loved to play with words. But he leaned forward to turn down the radio. "What can I do you for, Justin?"

"I want to find someone." *Don't ask me who it is,* I thought.

He didn't. Instead, his questions danced around the obvious one.

"Does this person *want* to be found?"

"I don't know."

"Well, if he— or she— *didn't* want to be found, would it be easy or difficult for them to hide?"

I couldn't visualize my dad crouched in some dark alleyway,

handing a wad of cash to some creepy low-life for a fake I.D. It wasn't too realistic.

"Difficult or easy?" I asked. "I'm not sure. But all I need is a first step, a direction to go in. What would you do?"

Mr. Dave leaned back in his chair and pondered the last donut, flipping it over with an oily index finger.

"I would try to figure out the last place this person was at," he said.

"How?"

You'll need to find the last person who saw him or her," he said. "Your trail will start there."

The morning bell rang. I grabbed my backpack and walked back down the hall, out into the bright morning sun. The campus was busy. I navigated my way through a basketball game and lined up for class behind my buddy Mark Looper.

Loop had blond, almost white, hair, which he styled with gel— a lot of it. Every day he came to school with a different look. That morning, his hair was purposely messed up, like he just walked through a car wash. The week before he had dreadlocks; two weeks back, a mohawk. But even more interesting than predicting what Loop's hair might look like the next day was the way he spoke to people.

"Hey, how's it going, Justin?" he asked. "What are you doing for lunch?"

Without waiting for a response, he threw out another question: "You gonna be at the card game we're having at 12:15?"

For the most part, Mark Looper only spoke in questions. I don't think I could do that if I tried. To him, it came naturally.

"I don't know right now, Loop," I said. "I might head over there after I eat. But thanks."

More kids cued up behind us. Mike was there, too, his face buried in a book thicker than a dictionary. The line moved up the ramp and into the classroom.

When I got inside, I tucked my backpack under my desk and tied off a strap to one of the legs. Kids loved to mess with each other's stuff, and I had to be extra careful, since the journal was in there.

Mike sat to my right. His book was *Shemlin's Guide to Biophysical Applications in Action, Third Edition*. I could have spent my whole life studying the first chapter and never understood a word.

Behind me was the exchange student from Pakistan, Bicsan Calp. Bicsan was quiet and kept to himself most of the time. But he was a cool guy, and one of Loop's lunchtime card players. He always had a small yellow rubber football with him. I never once saw him without it.

Behind Bicsan were the twins, Andy and Randy D'Amato. I think it was against school policy to have twins in the same class, but in first grade, when the principal wanted to separate them, their mother got upset. They had been together ever since. It was tough to tell them apart until around fourth grade, but then, Randy became heavier and a little taller, and Andy's hair got curlier.

One desk up was Ella Nguyen. In fourth grade, she wasn't very popular. Kids used to make fun of her, calling her "Ellaphant." But I guess that got old. And she got pretty. She was Vietnamese, with long, straight black hair and dark brown eyes. Ella's personality was a combination of intelligence and humor, but she wasn't stuck up about it. She hung around the popular kids at school, kids who were already planning on trying out for cheerleading or playing sports in middle school.

You had us read silently for ten minutes. The class let out an audible groan when you told us to take out our books for ten minutes of silent reading.

"The reason we read first thing in the morning," you said, "is that our brains are more fresh and active in the morning, especially for those of you who have had a good breakfast."

I could tell you were big on nutrition. You were probably horrified at all the soft drinks and chips kids were eating all hours of the day. I was as guilty as the next kid. I don't think broccoli, tofu, and sprout juice are ever going to catch on with our age group.

After silent reading, Mr. Croozer, the art teacher, craned his long neck inside the door. He came in once a week to do art with the kids, and had worked at our school since I was in third grade. You grabbed some papers and left.

Mr. Croozer was an interesting guy. He was tall and skinny, with a scraggly, black goatee and a pointy Adam's apple that bobbed up and down when he spoke. His hair was tied back into a tight ponytail. Mr. Croozer's deep-set eyes made it look like he was constantly worried, even when he was laughing. With his ripped blue jeans and swirly tie-dye shirts, "Mister C," as the students called him, looked like someone from the psychedelic hippie days of the 1960's.

The weirdest thing about Mr. Croozer was his toes. They were hairy. *Really* hairy. We knew because he always wore flip-flops at school. On each toe there was a thick patch of wiry black hair. And at the center of each patch, there was a flat, bald spot, like a little landing pad. Mr. Croozer's toes were like ten little nests, forever waiting for a tiny flock of toe-birds to return to them. My friends and I agreed that it was equal parts gross and fascinating. OK, maybe two-thirds gross. It was hard not to look at his toes, but we tried.

Mr. Croozer was very excited about art, and his mission was to get *us* excited about it. He usually failed.

"Today, class," he announced energetically in his nasally, high-pitched voice, "we are going to *finger*-paint!"

We stared at him silently, pondering his existence. He asked for volunteers to pass out supplies.

Ella and Bicsan volunteered to pour the paint. They filled large plastic cups with different colors and distributed them around the room. Mr. Croozer flip-flopped up to the front to give us directions.

"Folks," he said, twisting his goatee, "we're going to do something different today. I want you to paint something from your *heart*." He tapped his chest. We rolled our eyes.

"Forget about painting *something*. I want you to begin working with your materials and not stop to think about what you're doing." Scattered grunts and groans from the class. "Remember, you don't have to *make* anything," he continued. "I don't care about the final product. Just let your *hand* do what your *heart* tells it to, and then see what turns up on the paper." Vintage Mr. C.

What the heck— I decided to try it. I tried to empty my mind of all my thoughts. I didn't want anything I've been thinking about lately, like my dad, to influence my project. After a minute of concentration, all I saw was the piece of butcher paper in front of me.

I dipped my right index finger into the brown paint, and starting at the top of the paper, laid a thick, straight line down the middle of the paper, about a foot and a half long. I made a second, parallel line about four inches to the left of the first line. I didn't know what I was doing, but something was taking shape.

I re-dipped and made short vertical brown slashes in between the large brown lines. Suddenly, I felt like I knew what I was making; then, a second later, I had no idea. I went to the sink and washed the paint off my hands.

Green was next. I didn't know why. I grabbed a large empty cup, along with three small cups of green paint. I poured all the green paint into the big cup, filling it more than half full.

I lowered my entire right hand into the paint, letting the excess drip back into the cup. I pressed my hand down between the two brown lines at the top of the paper. I moved an inch down and re-pressed. I did that two more times before I had to re-dip.

A couple of kids came over to check out what I was doing. Randy told me it looked like a tree. Bicsan looked up from his painting of a three-dimensional cube and asked me, "What is it, Justin?"

"I don't know," I said. It was true, I didn't. But something familiar had begun to take shape on my paper, in the way that an image you'd see during the day might all of a sudden remind you of a dream you forgot you had.

After another couple of minutes, the entire space between the brown lines was filled with green handprints. There were ten of them. Mr. Croozer came over to my desk.

"Wow, Justin, right on," he said. "Way to use your materials, man. Are you finished?"

"Not yet," I said. "But close."

Looking at the paper, I could almost see what was missing. I felt a strange energy inside of me, like I was on the verge of discovering something that I once knew, a long time ago.

One more color. Andy had the red cup on his desk. There was only a little left, but it was all I needed. I made three short lines at the bottom of the paper, to the left of the two brown lines.

I looked at it. I knew right away that something was missing. All the colors were right, but it wasn't complete. I had seen the image before, though, or something very close to it.

CHAPTER 4:
The Socks

Lissy and I got home from school. Through the open back door, I saw Mom smoking a cigarette, her back toward me. She must have heard us come in, but she didn't turn around. Frank, Jr. was alone in the kitchen, watching cartoons from his highchair. The Tank was home early from work. I could tell right away that he was in his usual bad mood.

He ordered me and Alyssa into the laundry room. He had laid out straight rows of socks on top of the dryer. The Tank had sorted the socks by color, from dark to light, and by size, from small to large. Little cotton soldiers standing at attention.

"Justin and Alyssa," he began in a quiet voice that I knew wouldn't stay that way for long, "at approximately oh-seven-thirty this morning, I gathered this collection of socks from three different rooms around my house." Emphasis on *my*.

He held two socks up and waved them back and forth an inch from our faces, like a magician trying to hypnotize us. "Do these socks belong to either of you?"

Most of the socks were mine and one pair belonged to Alyssa, but I didn't want to give the Tank the satisfaction of admitting it. I would make him continue his interrogation. Lissy, maybe noticing I wasn't volunteering information, didn't say anything either.

Faced with uncooperative suspects, the Tank switched to what he thought would be a more persuasive tactic.

"Both of you," he yelled at us, his eyes filling with rage, "go to your room! You will stay there until you admit that these socks are *yours*!"

I heard the click of my mom's lighter as she fired up another cigarette and pretended not to hear. I wished she wouldn't let him yell at us like that. I wanted her to race into the house and get into the Tank's face, demanding that he back off from her kids. I wanted to see his shocked reaction as he realized that his reign of control had come to an end. But the Tank's voice reminded me that's all it was — a fantasy.

"What are you waiting for, a personal invitation? Get moving!"

We probably spent about two hours in the room. That was nothing; he had sent us there for a lot longer, and for lesser infractions. I had fallen asleep for a while. I was hungry.

Lissy was still asleep. Her hair had fallen in front of her face. She smiled slowly, eyelids twitching. I hoped she was having a good dream. She looked so peaceful when she slept.

I worried about how our life at the Tank's house was affecting her. She was younger than me and there was a lot that she didn't understand. I tried to answer her questions about Dad, but it wasn't easy, since I didn't really have any answers. Explaining the Tank's angry moods was almost as tough.

There had to be a limit to what a little kid could take. But Lissy was pretty tough. I knew she would make it through this. I would be there to help.

Later that night, I took out the journal. Despite my promise to write every day, I still hadn't even started. It was almost a shame to ruin those perfect, blank pages with words, but I knew I had to. Not that night though. Not yet. I closed the journal and ran my hands over the words, 'A CLEFT MIND'. What did it mean?

CHAPTER 5:
The Garden

It was the second morning after I got the journal. I was thinking about my painting, now hanging with the others in the class-room. I decided to visit Mr. Dave again, but on the way to his office, a campus supervisor asked me where I was going. I had to go back to the playground.

At recess, I tried again. I gave the secret knock, but there was no reply. I walked around to the other side of the building and looked inside the back door to the cafeteria's food prep area.

There was Mr. Dave, leaning back in a fold-up chair and laughing. The cafeteria ladies were laughing while he flirted with them. He turned around and saw me.

"Justin," he said, "What can I do you for?"

"I'll ask you later," I said.

I turned to leave, but Mr. Dave stood up, pushed in his chair, and walked outside, motioning me to follow him. We headed to-ward the small first grade garden.

He pulled some weeds and picked up a candy wrapper from the dirt near a lettuce plant. Mr. Dave liked to do stuff when he talked.

"Any luck on that person you were looking for?" He made

the conversation seem like no big deal, like we were talking about the weather or something. He continued his weed and trash patrol, tiptoeing through the carrot patch to nab a paper bag that was trying to blow away.

"No luck so far," I said. "But something interesting happened yesterday."

"Oh yeah? Tell me."

Mr. Dave picked his way through the garden while I described what happened during art class; how my hands seemed to almost work on their own, and how frustrating it was not to know the missing part of the painting.

We seemed to finish at the same time. He stood up, stretched, and slapped the dirt off his hands and on to his pants. Then he pulled a plastic trash bag out of his back pocket.

"You know, Justin," he said, "sometimes memories can be buried deep inside a person for a long time. Then, for some reason, those memories suddenly surface."

"Along with those memories (he stuffed a soda can and some empty water bottles into the bag) can come emotions that can cloud the memories, making them even more hazy and unclear."

We walked back up toward his office door. He found the right key out of a hundred clanging pretenders.

"It sounds to me like that painting might have triggered those lost memories," he said. "Now, you said you thought that you had seen this painting before. Do you remember when or where?"

"It's not a painting," I said. "At least, I don't think it is. When I see it in my mind, it's a lot bigger than it was on the butcher paper."

I'm not sure when I actually realized that— maybe just then, as I was telling it to Mr. Dave. We walked to his office. My eyes were slow to get used to the dark hallway.

Mr. Dave tossed the bag of recycling into a cardboard box. He dropped into his chair and swung his feet up onto the desk like he had done a thousand times before, his boots landing with a thud. A crooked pile of empty donut boxes swayed for a second but didn't fall. The bell that ended recess echoed back down the hall.

"Well, it sounds like you've got a couple of ways to go here, Justin," he said. "You have your painting. And we talked about finding the last person that saw… whoever it is. Let me know how things turn out."

My talk with Mr. Dave was interesting, but I was as far as ever from the truth. To really find out what happened to my dad, mysterious art projects and question-and-answer sessions with Mr. Dave weren't going to cut it. I would have to do something different. A lot different.

Mike and Mark were waiting as I emerged from the hallway. Mark's hair was combed forward and flat. If this was a new style, I must have missed the e-mail. Like always, Mark had questions, and as we walked toward class, he fired them at me like bullets.

"What do you do in there, Justin?" Mark asked. "Isn't that Mr. Dave's custodial room?"

"It's his office," I said. "We just talk, listen to music. It's pretty cool."

There was no need to get into much detail with Mark; it only caused him to ask more questions. But he did anyway.

"Can I go in there with you sometime?" he asked. "I mean, if it's OK with Mr. Dave?" I squinted as the sun reflected off of Mark's hair, momentarily blinding me.

"Yeah, sure, Loop. Sometime."

CHAPTER 6:
The Boxes

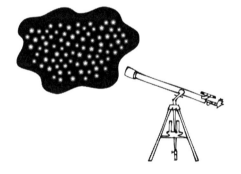

The Tank was still at work when Lissy and I got home. Mom was on the couch. Junior was next to her, napping. Drool was running from his mouth, forming a little puddle on the cushion. A talk show was on TV, the volume on mute.

Mom used to greet us at the door with a hug, or ask us how our day went. I couldn't be sure, but I thought she might have nodded in our direction. Or maybe it was just wishful thinking.

I made peanut butter and jelly sandwiches and poured glasses of milk for me and Sis. We sat at the kitchen table.

"Lissy, what did your teacher give you for homework?"

"Thee gabe us tum taples," she said.

"What?"

"Thee gabe us times tables!"

"Sis, don't talk with your mouth full," I told her.

"My mouf ithn't fool," she said.

She smiled, displaying the brown and purple remains of her sandwich, and opened up her backpack, pulling out a page of multiplication problems and a times table chart.

"I'm supposed to finish my math tonight," she said, "but I'm not good at my times tables. Can you help me?"

"Sure." We started with the easy numbers, the twos and threes. She gained a little confidence.

I brought our dirty dishes to the sink. If the kitchen was dirty when the Tank came home, his reaction would make the sock incident seem like nothing. I even made sure the dish sponge was aligned with the edge of the sink. I dried the plates and glasses, put them away, and then wiped down the table for crumbs.

"Sis, start on your fours now," I told her. "Use the multiplication chart. I'll check back with you in a bit."

There was something I had always been curious about: Where did all my dad's stuff go? The day I got home and found out that he was gone, I ran to his closet. It was empty. Not even a hanger was left. I couldn't believe that in only a few hours, my dad could have packed up everything he owned. There had to be *something* left behind. With the Tank still not home, I had a few minutes to look around the house.

I walked down the hall to the last door on the left. It was one of the Tank's "future use" rooms. I had never been inside. I had been too scared of getting caught. I stood in front of the door and thought about the consequences. All bad. I turned the knob slowly, and pushed the door open.

It looked like some creepy display at a museum. In the center of the room, the Tank had stacked brown moving boxes. The boxes had been pushed against each other to form a large cube, about eight feet tall, wide, and deep, like a giant brown Rubik's Cube. Each box had a white label stuck to the center of the side that faced out, its contents written in perfect capital letters.

I walked around the structure. I felt like I was looking at a diagram of the Tank's brain. I wondered why his mind worked like it did. Why did he have to stack the boxes so perfectly, to stick all the labels in the exact center of each box? Why did he print like a computer? I read some of the labels: HOME OFFICE SUPPLIES, MILITARY PAPERWORK, TAX INFO 2010.

There was one box that was different. It was a level up from the bottom of the stack and at the corner farthest from the door. It was smaller, and I couldn't see a label on it. It wasn't normal for the Tank to allow this outcast. I wrapped my fingers around the box's bent flap.

A thought came to me. "*Justin, this is really stupid. The Tank could be home any second.*" I pushed it out of my mind. Working the box back and forth, I pulled it out of its space without causing a landslide. I walked back to the door and listened. Nothing.

There were four words written on one of the flaps: *Danny Tyme's Personal Stuff.* I couldn't remember what my dad's writing looked like, but it was too sloppy to be the Tank's work.

I hadn't seen his name written in a long time. I closed my eyes and imagined that the box contained the clue I needed to find out what happened. I unfolded the flaps and looked inside.

There was a stack of envelopes and a box of paper clips. That was all. So much for the clue. I picked up the envelopes and smelled them. They smelled like envelopes. But they were my dad's envelopes.

I put them back. I was about to close up the box when a little flash of white caught my eye. It was a card, stuck under a bottom flap. I pulled it out and read:

Danny Tyme
Structural Engineering and Architecture
ARCH-TECH ENGINEERING
2104 Persing Avenue
Bent Valley, CA 54321
arch-tech@build-it.com
(408) 555-1234

I heard Mr. Dave's advice in my head: *"I would try to figure out the last place this person was at."* Maybe it was his work?

Then I heard something else: the front door opening. The Tank was home. And I was in a room I wasn't supposed to be in, looking at stuff I wasn't supposed to be looking at.

It was too late to run. There was only one other option.

Hide.

I jammed the card into my pocket. I tried to shove the box back into the stack, but it didn't fit anymore. The weight of the other boxes had shifted and there was no longer enough room. The Tank's keys jingled as he hung them up on the hook behind the front door.

He was coming down the hall. I prayed he wouldn't stop. The footsteps grew louder. I sat behind the stack of boxes, holding my dad's box on my lap. My life as I knew it would be over if he found me. The footsteps stopped in front of the door. Like an idiot, I had left it open. His stare felt like a laser beam as he scanned the room.

"Justin."

His voice was calm, but underneath it I sensed great anger. I wasn't sure if he knew I was in the room, so I gambled and stayed silent.

"Alyssa," he bellowed back toward the living room, "where's your brother?"

"I dunno," she said sleepily. "He left me after the snack."

There was silence for maybe ten more seconds. It felt like an hour. The door closed. I heard the Tank walk down the hall and go into his bedroom.

I could breathe again. I took the box and walked silently back down the hall and into my room, where I pushed the envelopes and paper clips as far under my mattress as I could. Then I pulled apart my dad's box and stuffed the flattened cardboard into my backpack to throw away at school. If the Tank saw the pieces in the trash he'd be suspicious and might investigate.

There was always the chance that he would examine the stack of boxes and notice the empty space, but there was nothing I could do about that.

I went back to the living room. Alyssa was on the couch next to Mom, sleeping. My little brother was sitting on the floor in front of them, trying to eat his favorite book, "Big Horsey Needs a Friend."

"Junior," I asked him, "do you want me to read to you?" He smiled up at me, crinkling his nose and displaying a shiny white bottom tooth.

"Bah bah," he told me, pointing the book at me. Maybe he was trying to say "book." I knew Junior was smart. Must have taken after his older brother. I picked him up off the floor and sat down at the table with him on my lap.

I read him "Big Horsey Needs a Friend." It was about a lonely horse that lived on a farm. Because he was new to the farm, none of the other animals wanted to be his friend. While I read and turned pages, Junior made funny noises and pointed to the different animals. Finally, an insomniac owl made friends with Big Horsey, and the story finished with the predictably happy ending.

I wished Junior was older already and could talk. I thought about how much fun it would be to have a *brother* to do things with. I put Junior down and went to my room.

Junior's book reminded me of a night a few years back when we had a campout in the backyard. I was pretty young, and Alyssa was a toddler. My dad put up a tent, lit a campfire, and we roasted marshmallows. When it got dark, I helped my dad set up the telescope. It was a perfect night for stargazing. There was no moon and the sky was pitch black.

My dad asked me to try and find the dimmest star I could. I had to ask him what "dimmest" meant. I looked through the telescope at clusters of bright stars, thinking the dim ones would be hidden in there somewhere.

Finally, I gave up. I told my dad I couldn't find a dim star; they all looked so bright. He said to me, "Search a darker sky." I focused the telescope on a black patch almost directly above us. And there it was: a tiny speck of light barely visible through the eyepiece.

The telescope is gone now, and so is my dad. But sometimes, on a clear night, I look up and try to find that little star.

CHAPTER 7:
The Building

It was the third day since I got the journal and it was raining hard. I climbed aboard the bus and asked Mike for the window seat. I was nervous about my plan. I wanted to tell him, but I couldn't.

It was a rough ride. Twice, the back tires lost their grip and the bus skidded a little, but the driver didn't seem worried. Mike was reading another book, "Organic Chemistry for the Gifted Mind." Before I could read a few sentences, he turned the page. If I had even one quarter of Mike's brainpower, I might have already found my dad.

The bus swung in to the parking lot. I bent down behind the seat and pretended like I was looking for something. The kids filed off the bus and I peeked up to see if the driver was looking in the rear-view mirror. He wasn't. I stayed hidden behind my seat as the bus engine roared back to life. The air brakes hissed and the bus pulled away from the curb. I knew where it was going: The bus yard downtown, a few blocks from the business district.

I sat on the floor of the bus with my chin on my knees, the vibration of the engine shaking my legs. I had fifteen minutes to wonder if I was doing the right thing.

Something clicked inside of me the day before, when I was reading to Junior. I realized that, pretty soon, he would be the one asking questions about what happened to our family. And I wanted to be able to tell him. I was his older brother. If not me, then who?

I had big doubts about what I was doing. But I decided to do it anyway. I hoped Alyssa wouldn't say anything when she figured out I wasn't at school.

The bus pulled into the yard, braked hard, and stopped. The engine shuddered, and then it was still. The automatic door opened and the bus tilted slightly as the driver walked down the stairs.

I looked out the window. The school busses were lined up in aisles and rows, like students sitting at their desks. Staying low, I slinked to the front of the bus and stepped off.

I didn't know downtown well enough to do it on my own. I needed help from someone — or a map. The map option sounded better, since an adult might wonder what a kid was doing alone, during school hours.

As, I was leaving the yard, I got lucky: a map literally blew against my leg. It was soggy, but when I unfolded it, it was just what I needed: a block-by-block diagram of the business district.

I took out the business card and checked the address. I tried to find Arch-Tech by first finding the bus yard on the map. I still couldn't pinpoint Persing Avenue. There was a triangle-shaped area on the map that was too mushy to read. Persing was there, somewhere. At least I knew what direction to go in.

I was worried, because I was skipping school, something I had never done without permission. But I was excited as well, because I had never been on my own, with no one knowing where I was.

A man lying on the sidewalk asked me for money. I ignored

him. A group of women power-walked toward me, pushing covered strollers. I turned away from them as they passed. I knew the chance of being recognized out there was about zero, but why take chances?

I liked downtown. The way the skyscrapers followed me when I looked up. The clanging of trolley bells. The scream of police sirens. The echo of car horns.

But I didn't like being splashed with water when a car drove by, close to the curb. Or the three seconds the signal gave me to cross the street. Or the unidentifiable gross stuff on the sidewalk.

After a few blocks, I knew that I was near the business district. Men in suits hurried past me, cell phones pressed to their ears. A woman in a bright blue dress carrying a brief case slammed shut her car door, having a heated argument with herself. Then I saw the wireless earpiece.

A homeless guy wearing filthy Superman pajamas pushed a shopping cart past the woman, singing a song in a language I didn't recognize. He stopped suddenly, raised his hands in the air, and laughed hysterically. Three men walked past him like he wasn't even there. Downtown, people only notice what they want to.

Persing Avenue had to be close. I needed to ask someone. There was a newsstand on the corner. I ducked underneath its green cloth umbrella. An older man was there, in an ink-smudged green apron, humming and counting quarters. The raindrops made popping sounds on the fabric overhang above me.

"Excuse me, sir," I asked politely. "Can you tell me where I might find Persing Avenue?" He looked across at me and furrowed his brow.

"Why you lookin' for Persing, boy?"

I wanted to tell him, "None of your business," but that wouldn't get me anywhere. Instead, I got creative.

"I'm supposed to meet my dad at his job. It's 'Take Your Kid to Work Day'." He didn't say anything for a second.

"What's your dad do for a livin'?"

"He's an architect," I said. "He designs buildings and stuff."

The man gave me a suspicious look. Maybe he was wondering why a parent wouldn't have made sure their kid had directions in the first place.

"Alright, boy. Make a left down there at the corner and go three blocks. Good luck."

The man went back to counting quarters. I didn't like being dishonest with him, but a little white lie every now and then wouldn't hurt. Sometimes it was necessary.

I walked a block when I realized that my backpack was getting wet. I checked a trashcan for something to cover it with. I pulled out a white plastic shopping bag. As I shook the water from it, a woman who looked a lot like the poodle she was walking gave me a disgusted scowl. Her dog gave me the same look. And that from a species of animal whose favorite way of communicating is butt sniffing.

Before I slid the bag over my backpack, I pulled out the cardboard pieces from my dad's box and stuffed them in the trash. I walked the remaining two and a half blocks, hit Persing, and started reading addresses. It began to rain harder. I ducked under a hotel overhang to wait it out.

I looked across the street. There it was. The building was

small; it didn't fit in with its taller neighbors. A small black and white sign read:

ARCH-TECH ENGINEERING
2104 Persing

My dad had worked there. Like a movie clip playing in my head, I see him. He's running across the street, holding a folded up newspaper under his arm, a cup of coffee in his hand. He swings the door open and disappears inside.

I slicked back my wet hair, jogged across the street, and pulled on the door. A security guard sat behind a desk in the corner of a wide, marble-floored lobby. He saw me and put his magazine down.

"Young man, what can I do for you?" He seemed friendly.

"I'm here to see my dad," I said. "He works here." I put my backpack down and looked around, trying to seem confident.

"Well, first off, my name's Leonard. I'm the new security guard here. What's your name?"

"Justin," I said.

"OK, Justin, so what's your dad's name?" he asked. "I'll call upstairs and tell him you're here."

"I doubt you'll find his name on any list. He's just been hired recently. He transferred in from another company." Right away I regretted not telling him the truth. But I wanted to get upstairs, and I thought that would give me the best chance.

"Well, I'm new as well! I know how tough a new assignment can be. Tell me his name and we'll give it a try."

"It's— Smith. John Smith." It was a long shot. But with that being such a common name, I thought I might get lucky.

"John Smith, huh?" he asks. "OK..."

The guard studied the phone list, repeating the name a few times as he ran down the page with his finger: "John Smith, John Smith. Here we are: J. Smith, extension 94." He picked up the phone and dialed.

"Hi, Mr. Smith?" he said, smiling up at me. "This is Leonard downstairs in Security. I got a kid down here, says he's your son. You want me to send him up?" There was a pause while he listened.

"Uh-huh, I see. Yes. OK. Thank you."

By the tone of his voice, I could tell that my plan had failed. He hung up the phone.

"OK, little buddy, you're good to go. Take the elevator around the corner. Go to the second floor. He's in his office."

The words didn't register. I'm not sure how, but it worked! I covered up my excitement, grabbed my backpack, and started walking.

"Thanks, Leonard," I said.

"No problem. Have a good one."

The elevator doors were open. I pressed '2'. The doors closed. Huge photographs of bridges and skyscrapers were on the walls, I guessed ones that Arch-Tech had designed. The elevator lurched to a stop.

It was busy upstairs. Cubicles were spaced throughout the

office in what seemed like random patterns. Employees streamed past each other. Some people sat at tall, slanted desks, using tools I didn't recognize. Others were typing on laptops or talking on the phone. It looked like everyone had something to do.

But I didn't know what to do. How was I supposed to find out anything about my dad? I didn't know where to turn. The smell of coffee and donuts reminded me of Mr. Dave's office. The smell of sharpened pencils reminded me of the Principal's office, a place I might be visiting soon.

I was maybe thirty feet from the elevator when I noticed a man motioning toward me from behind a window on the far side of the big room. I looked around to see if there was someone else he was waving to. He pointed at me and nodded a "Yes, you!"

I got to his office. The nameplate on the door had "Jerry Smith, CFO" engraved into it. I was about to knock when a deep voice from behind it said, "Enter."

The man was sitting in a big black chair behind a large black desk. He had on a dark suit with a red tie. His stern face had wrinkles around the eyes, and his mustache was a couple shades darker than his slicked-back grey hair. The gold watch on his wrist looked like it cost a lot of money.

"Sit down," he said.

I did, in a small chair on my side of the desk. The visitor's chair was lower than the one he was sitting in, so I had to look up at him.

"Young man, I just got a call from the guard downstairs," he said angrily. "He told me that my *son* was here to see me. I don't have any children. What the hell is going on?"

It was time to tell the truth. I was lucky to have gotten as far as I had. I pulled the business card from my pocket.

"First of all, I'm sorry about lying to the security guard," I said. "My name is Justin, and I'm looking for my dad. His name is Danny Tyme, and I think he used to work here. I found this card."

I handed Mr. Smith the card. He leaned back in his chair and studied it.

"*Danny Tyme, Structural Engineering and Architecture*," he said. "That's strange."

"What is?" I asked.

"Well, I've worked at Arch-Tech for almost eleven years now," he said. "I worked my way up from the very bottom of this company. In fact, I used to mop floors downstairs at night."

Mr. Smith tapped the card on the desk a few times. Then, looking straight at me, he ripped the card into pieces and dumped them into the trashcan next to the desk.

"I even worked security for a year," Mr. Smith said, his voice getting louder. "And in all my time here, I've never even *heard* of a Danny Tyme. So I don't know who you are, or what you're trying to pull, but I suggest that you get the hell out of here before I call the police and have you arrested for trespassing and truancy!"

I was in shock. I stood up, picked up my backpack and left his office, quietly closing the door behind me. As I walked back down the walkway, I felt Mr. Smith's eyes burning a hole in my back.

I got to the elevator and turned around. He was still watching me. I pushed the "down" button. It felt like forever while I waited for the doors to open. Finally, they did.

A man was already inside. I moved aside to let him exit, but he didn't move.

"I'm going down," he whispered.

I thought that was weird, since he had to have come from downstairs already. The building had only two stories. But what was even weirder was that the man was pushed up against the side of the elevator wall, like he didn't want to be seen.

I didn't really care, though. My talk with Mr. Smith had sucked all the energy out of me. I got in and the doors closed. I moved toward the panel to hit the button, but it was already lit. The elevator started to move.

I looked up at the man. He had curly brown afro-type hair and wire rim glasses that framed a bony, freckle-filled face. Unlike most of the workers in the office, he was dressed casually, in jeans and a button-down shirt. Third weird thing: he was really sweaty. Then, without warning, the man reached over and pushed the emergency stop button and the elevator jerked to a halt.

"What are you doing?" I asked. All I could think of was getting out of the elevator and yelling for Leonard's help.

"We only have a second," he said. "I have information about your father. We can't talk now — I've got to get back upstairs. Meet me in a half-hour at Skippy's Coffee Shop on West Benton. Find an empty booth. Now get out of here."

"But wait, who — "

"There's no time!"

The man released the lock on the elevator and the doors slid open. I got out and turned around to look at him, but he had moved back against the side again. Leonard was still at his desk in the lobby.

"So, partner, was your dad glad to see you?"

"Oh, yeah," I said. "It was great. Thanks a lot."

CHAPTER 8:
The Restaurant

I stood outside the Arch-Tech entrance, underneath the canopy. I was trying to figure out how to feel after my encounter with Mr. Smith and the stranger in the elevator. My hands were trembling while I looked for West Benton on my map. It was a little black line parallel to Persing, a few blocks over.

I dodged the miniature waterfalls that ran off the overhangs and jumped over tiny lakes. Even though I had plenty of time, I walked quickly, daydreaming about what the man might say. Did he know my dad? Did he know what happened to him, or where he was?

I almost missed the entrance to Skippy's. Only a small vertical sign flashing blue neon letters stuck out from the wall. I went inside. It was dark and almost empty. Elevator music played. An older lady walked up to me, wiping her hands on a dishrag.

"Welcome to Skippy's, son," she said in a crackly, high-pitched southern accent. "Sit wherever you'd like."

I found a booth at the back of the restaurant, by the restrooms. I put my backpack under the table. With my back to the wall, I could see the entrance. The lady appeared again, handed me a menu, and gave me a smile full of smoky-brown teeth. The deep lines on her face told me she'd been at this for a while.

"Mah name is Dolores, hun. Why don't ya take a minute to look at the menu? I'll be back in a flash."

I checked my pocket for money: four dollars and thirty-three cents. That wouldn't buy me a full meal, but I could afford a couple of sides. Dolores returned, and I ordered a bowl of cereal, some toast, and water.

"Hi, I'm Sebastian Seely."

Startled, I looked up to find the man from the elevator, extending his hand for me to shake. He squeezed mine way too hard.

"Hey, thanks for coming," I said. "Have a seat." He took a quick look around and then slid in across from me.

"What's good here?" he asked, picking up a menu. I couldn't believe he was talking about food when he claimed to know something about my dad, but I played it cool.

"I've never been here before. I ordered breakfast."

Dolores brought my food. Our silence continued while Mr. Seely looked at the menu. I checked my bill and figured out how much of a tip I could leave. Twenty-three cents. When I looked up, I could see Mr. Seely's hands shaking. He was even sweatier than he had been in the elevator.

Dolores returned to take his order, a double cheeseburger and fries. She scooped up my bill with the cash on top of it, gave me a courtesy smile, and walked away. Mr. Seely looked around the restaurant, then across at me.

"I was in the same workgroup as your father," he said quietly. "He was a remarkable engineer. Just the way he thought about things, how he was able to tackle problems from different perspectives. Danny was light years ahead of the rest of us. He was amazing."

"Mister Seely —"

"Call me Sebastian, please."

"OK, Sebastian, so, why did Jerry Smith lie to me?" I asked. "He told me that he had never heard of Danny Tyme."

He leaned back in the booth. He started to speak, but stopped when Dolores came over and dropped off his food. Sebastian pulled apart the burger and dumped about half a bottle of ketchup on to the patty. Then he delivered a separate, even larger pile next to his fries. He took a massive bite, chewing for what seemed like forever. After wiping some ketchup off his chin, he spoke.

"Our workgroup had four engineers," he said. "I was one of them, as was your dad. There was another guy, Darren. And Jerry Smith was the group leader, responsible for everything the group produced."

"What did you guys do?" I asked him while he smacked the bottom of the ketchup bottle. "I mean, what did you make?"

Sebastian nodded his head at me like he was saying, *good question.* But he didn't answer it right away. Instead he sunk an armada of fries into his red sea of ketchup.

"From the start, the four engineers were kind of like our own small company, working separately from the rest of the employees on the floor. We were given several challenging and exciting projects, and we worked well together."

"Then, our group was contracted out," he said. "That means we were really working for another company. Only Jerry Smith knew exactly who they were. And by that time, Smith was in management, so we didn't ask too many questions. We were all making pretty good money, so why rock the boat, right?"

"Anyway, back to your question. Our focus was to examine

ways in which common construction materials— like brick, steel, and wood— could be combined to help improve a building's structural integrity."

"I followed you up to the point where you talked about the brick and steel," I said. "Then, you lost me."

"Look," he said, "I'll show you." He scanned the table for something that wasn't there.

"Go up to the front counter and grab a bunch of toothpicks," he told me.

Toothpicks? I walked up to the front counter and pressed the lever on the toothpick holder twenty times or so. Dolores was at the register. She tilted her head to the side like a puppy and looked at me, but didn't say anything.

I came back and dumped the toothpicks on the table, just as Sebastian was finishing his last ketchup-drenched bite of burger. For a skinny guy, the man could eat. He pushed the dirty dishes aside.

"Now, we need straws," he said. I got up again. Dolores didn't seem to mind when I asked her for a handful of straws.

Sebastian worked quickly. He pushed the pile of toothpicks to one side of the table, and moved the straws to the other side. Then he used a butter knife to cut up his last french fry into little pieces. I had no idea what all this was for.

"When a large structure is built, say, a skyscraper or bridge," Sebastian explained, "materials arrive at the construction site sep-arately." He gestured toward the two piles.

"Let's say that the toothpicks are the cement and that the straws are the steel. Workers construct the building piece-by-piece and part-by-part."

"First," he said, "cement workers pour the concrete foundation." To demonstrate, Sebastian laid down seven or eight toothpicks parallel to each other.

"Then, metal workers build a steel frame." He cut two straws into four equal pieces, and then stabbed pieces of the french fry onto the ends of them, forming them together into a square. He then placed the square over the toothpicks.

"Somehow," Sebastian said, "your dad was able to combine these materials on a *molecular* level. This would allow components for the buildings to be prefabricated — made at the factory."

"Molecular?" I asked him. "That sounds like chemistry."

"It *is* chemistry, Justin," Sebastian said, his eyes lighting up. "Danny worked for months on something he called C-Metal. Everyone at Arch-Tech, including me, thought he was crazy. For years, scientists had tried to change the actual structure of materials, but with little success."

"Have you ever heard of alchemy? No? Well, suffice it to say that your dad was trying to reinvent the engineering wheel."

"Jerry pushed the group hard. It was a stressful time at Arch-Tech. Only your dad seemed to believe that it could actually be done. He worked long hours, including at home on his computer."

"Then, one morning, your dad came into our group's 10 a.m. meeting with a stack of equations and a huge smile on his face. He had done it. We were awestruck."

"So, what is this C-Metal stuff?" I asked Sebastian.

"C-Metal stands for cement metal," he said. "If I were a genius, like your dad, I could probably explain in detail what it is. What I do know is that he found a way to make molecules attach to each other and form structures that, strung together by the billions, are incredibly strong."

Sebastian grabbed four toothpicks off the table, and, holding them together, slid them inside a straw.

"It's incredible stuff," he said, holding the toothpick-stuffed straw in front of me. "Easy to make, four times as strong as steel, but only *half* as expensive," he said. "And, ironically, that was the problem."

"What problem?" I asked him. "It sounds like my dad invented the perfect stuff."

"The problem," Sebastian said, "was that your dad would only agree to release the chemical recipe for C-Metal to the company that had hired Arch-Tech on one condition."

"Which was what?"

"His condition was that C-Metal not be used for any military product," he said. "He was totally against the idea that the technology he developed might be used to harm others." Sebastian was silent as Dolores cleared our dishes.

"Why would the military be interested in C-Metal?" I asked.

"I think Jerry Smith, our group leader, saw dollar signs," he said. "He found out from a well-placed friend that the military was developing a new type of missile-transport vehicle, and that they would jump at the chance to obtain C-Metal, pay huge money for it."

"Think about it, Justin," he said. "A military vehicle that's light-weight but *four times as strong* as anything they'd ever had.

And dirt-cheap to produce. Can't you just imagine the Pentagon bigwigs frothing at the mouth?"

"Say, why don't we walk for a little bit, work off our food?" he asked, getting up from the table. "I'll tell you the rest outside."

It was still raining. Sebastian walked quickly, but I kept up. I couldn't shake the habit of trying to miss the cracks on the sidewalk. Didn't want to break my mother's back.

"It turns out that Jerry Smith's well-placed 'friend' was an employee of the company that hired us for the project. What that means is that the workgroup that your dad and I belonged to had actually been working for the military the whole time. It had been prearranged by Jerry and that friend of his."

"What did my dad do when he found out?" I asked.

"Danny was pissed. Jerry asked him for the pass phrase that would tell the computer to run the program and produce the C-Metal chemical recipe. Your dad refused. I believe that the pass phrase was actually a derivative of the recipe itself, and as a result, the chance of Jerry finding it on his own was something close to one in one septillion. That's the number one followed by 24 zeros, Justin. You'd have a better chance of winning the next one hundred lotteries in a row than discovering that pass phrase."

"Without the pass phrase, C-Metal would only exist in Danny's mind, as an incredible idea. But if Jerry and his military buddy could make it a reality, they'd be rich beyond their wildest dreams."

We walked past a bus stop bench packed with people. My brain snapped back to school for a second. I wondered if I was in trouble for not being there. Sebastian stopped at the same newsstand I was at earlier and bought a paper. He rolled it up and stuffed it into his back pocket.

The man in the green apron looked across at him. "You must be Dad, right?"

"What's that?" Sebastian asked.

"Your son, he found you."

Sebastian looked back at me.

"Don't ask," I said.

"Soon after all this happened, your dad confided in me," Sebastian said. "I think he felt that he could trust me. That's how I know what little I know." We crossed the street.

"Nothing Jerry Smith could say or do would change your dad's mind," he said. "Danny was threatened with being fired, then with being sued. I don't think your dad's problem was entirely with the military; it was also that he had been lied to— deceived."

"Justin, I need to get back to work," he said. "I've told you almost everything I know. There are two more quick things. After Jerry Smith's threats against your father didn't work, things seemed to calm down for a couple of days. Then, a man showed up at Arch-Tech. He was a big guy. Had on a baseball cap. He wore blue sweats and a white tank top. I saw him meet with Jerry Smith in his office. Then he went into Danny's cubicle."

"I don't know what the man said to your dad, but a few minutes later, they left Arch-Tech together," Sebastian said. "That was the last time I ever saw Danny Tyme. He never came back to work."

"Then, a few weeks after your dad's disappearance, I was looking through my desk and I found this." He pulled his wallet out and removed a small card.

"Danny must have stuck it in my desk; I'm not sure when," he said, handing me the card. "He trusted me to get it to you; I didn't want to let him down." I folded my hand around the card without looking at it.

I felt a mix of excitement, optimism, and a little anxiety, similar to when I saw the label on my dad's box in the Tank's storage room. But I was also angry.

"Why didn't you try to find me?" I asked Sebastian. "I haven't seen my dad in three years!"

"Justin, I had a good reason. He also left another card in my desk."

"Well, what did it say?" I asked him.

"It had seven words on it," he said. "The first four words were, 'Let him find you'. For whatever reason, your dad wanted you to find me, not the other way around. Would you have expected me to go against his wishes?"

I took a breath. "No, I guess not. It's just been a little stressful for me today."

"Totally understandable," Sebastian said.

"So besides, 'Let him find you', what were the other three words?" I asked him.

"Well, those were the three I didn't understand. Maybe you will. Your dad wrote, 'A Cleft Mind'."

A Cleft Mind. The journal. My dad. They were connected. I had the weirdest sensation just then. I was floating above Sebastian and myself, watching us talk.

The first card! I had squeezed it so hard that it was mashed into my palm. I peeled my fingers from it and looked.

My drawing from art class. The two brown lines, the ten green handprints, the three red marks. I couldn't believe it. I felt dizzy. Things got dark for a second. I closed my eyes. When I opened them, Sebastian looked worried.

"Are you OK?"

"Yeah, I think so. It's just— I wasn't expecting to see this again," I said, holding up the card.

"Again?" Sebastian asked. "What do you mean? You've seen it before?"

"I'm not sure. I painted something like it."

"Your painting matches the card? That's weird."

"Can you remember anything else about the man who left with my dad?" I asked. "Anything besides the sweats and tank top?" Sebastian thought for a moment.

"Wow, it was a few years ago; things are a bit blurry. Let's see...OK, the man had a tattoo. I saw it when he and Danny walked by my cube on the way to the elevator. The tattoo was green, with some kind of... yellowish something in the middle. I didn't really see it too clearly. I think— there might have been a number— maybe 90 something?"

It sounded a lot like the Tank's tattoo.

How many guys with a look and body type similar to the Tank would also have a green and yellow tattoo with a number on it? Maybe plenty. Could be that it was something common in the military; a lot of ex-soldiers could have it.

I needed to get back home and make my mom talk to me. She had to have known that my dad's disappearance had to do with his work— he must have told her *something*. What couldn't she tell me? I reached for my backpack to put the card inside— my backpack! I left it at Skippy's!

I took off in a dead sprint. After half a block I turned around to yell, "Thank you!" to Sebastian, but I couldn't see him. I jaywalked across streets, crossed against red lights, and squeezed past people on the sidewalk. I was out of breath when I got back to the restaurant. Dolores was at the register, handing change to a customer.

"Well, you're back," Dolores said, wiping the counter down. I couldn't tell if she was being welcoming or sarcastic.

"Hey, I left my backpack here. Did you find it?" She used the puppy head tilt on me again.

"Nope," she answered back. "Haven't even cleaned the table yet. Go have a look-see if you want."

I walked back to the table and looked underneath. Yes! I grabbed the backpack. It was time to get home. Passing the register, I nodded my thanks to Dolores.

"Hey, hun," she said, "someone was in here a few minutes ago, lookin' for ya."

"Looking for *me*?" No one knew I was here besides Sebastian. "Are you sure?"

"Sure as death and taxes," she said. "Described you perfect. He was a real big guy, shaved head. Left you something in case you came back."

She reached under the register shelf and handed me something.

A blue sticky note.

BOY,

WE NEED TO TALK. STAY HERE.

YOU KNOW WHO.

The letters. I knew them well. Straight and perfect, like a machine.

How did he know I had been at Skippy's? Unless Jerry Smith had called him when I showed up at Arch-Tech. And that would mean the man who left with my dad three years ago really was the Tank.

He would count on me taking the city bus back home. I had to find a different way. I decided to take a chance back at the school bus yard. I had to talk to my mom before the Tank found me. I needed to know what she knew. Needed to make her tell me.

I ran back to the yard. Only a few buses were left, parked parallel to each other in the far end of the lot. I didn't see anybody, but I heard one of the buses' engines running.

I pushed on the doors and they gave way easily, but closing them was tougher. I couldn't pull them together. I knew the driver might be suspicious if he saw the doors open. Then I remembered the button that the bus driver used.

I walked to the back of the bus and got down into the same position I was in on my trip downtown from school, tucking my backpack between my legs. Déjà vu. All I could do was wait.

CHAPTER 9:
The Twist

I felt the driver get on. A few turns and the bus left the yard, picked up speed and seemed to stay straight. I had no idea where it was going. After maybe fifteen minutes, the floor shuddered as the driver braked and the bus came to a stop. I poked my head up and watched her walk up to a house I didn't recognize.

It might have been my only opportunity to get off without being noticed. I was about three miles from my house. That was lucky— I could have been 20 miles away. From where I was, it would take maybe an hour to walk home.

While I walked, my head swirled with thoughts: the cards, the painting, my mom…the pattern of my footsteps was so automatic that, before I knew it, I had walked for 45 minutes.

About a mile from my house, I tripped on an uneven section of the sidewalk and fell, twisting my ankle. At first, I didn't think it was bad. The next house down had a short rock wall along the front yard. I limped over to it, sat down, and took off my shoe and sock.

Mistake. The ankle began puffing up. I put my sock and shoe back on and tightened up the laces to try and control the swelling. My shoes looked weird, with loose laces on one and tight ones on the other. Two police cars sped by, lights on but no sirens. I figured there was a car wreck.

I walked another block and my foot was throbbing. I tried putting my weight on the other foot, but it didn't help. At a bus stop bench, I took off my shoe and sock again and stuffed them into my backpack. I sat there and waited. I couldn't think of anything else to do.

"Hey Justin, hop on!"

My luck continued! Mr. Dave pulled his motorcycle over to the curb, smiling and gunning the accelerator. I wasn't ready for the big motorcycle ride yet, but I had no choice. I stood up and I limped over to the bike. Mr. Dave looked down at my foot.

"One of those days, huh?" he asked me over the rumble of the engine.

"Yep."

I struggled to climb on to the back. Mr. Dave reached down to the storage compartment and pulled out a helmet.

"Put this on. You're gonna need it."

It sounded like a warning. I put the helmet on and pulled the chinstrap tight enough to cut off blood flow to my brain.

"Where you headed, home?" he asked me, checking the rear-view mirror for traffic.

"Yeah, it's about a mile up," I said, while I tried to figure out where to put my feet.

"OK, hold on!" he yelled back at me.

Mr. Dave gunned the engine and eased the big bike back on to the street, swerved around a car, and accelerated so fast that I had to hold on to the back of his jacket to keep from being thrown off.

I wasn't scared. My helmet's visor was up, and the cool, fresh air felt good against my face. Another police car raced past us. After a couple of minutes, I motioned to Mr. Dave to make a few left turns, then a right. I tapped on his shoulder and signaled him to pull over. He slowed down and pulled the bike to the curb.

We were about a block from the Tank's place. A bunch of police cars were parked at crazy angles in front of the house. I had no idea what was going on there, but I felt sick to my stomach. Mr. Dave cut the engine. I climbed off the bike and he pushed it forward onto the kickstand.

"I wonder what's going on over there?" he asked, stepping on to the sidewalk.

"I'm not sure."

"That isn't your place, is it?"

"No, I'm two houses down from there," I lied. "Probably just the crazy neighbor again."

I unhooked the chinstrap and pulled the helmet off. Mr. Dave took it from me and got back on the bike. Looking down at my foot again, he asked, "Are you gonna be OK?"

For a second I changed my mind. I wanted to tell him about C-Metal, about how I thought Jerry Smith and the Tank might be working together, that it was the Tank's house that the cops were in front of. But I couldn't.

"I'll be OK," I told him. "Thanks for the lift. I guess I'll see you at school tomorrow?"

"OK. Take care of that foot," he said. "Ice the heck out of it, and keep it elevated. And you better think about staying home if it still looks that bad in the morning."

"Will do," I said. "Thanks again."

Mr. Dave pushed the bike off the stand, and with one solid kick, fired the engine back to life. He gave me the "thumbs up" sign. Then he was gone. The rumble of the bike's engine faded away, and then all I heard was the chatter of the police radios.

I needed to find out what was going on at the house. Were all the cops there just because of me? Or was my mom in trouble? I limped closer to the Tank's place and hid behind a fence. The red lights from the police cars flickered and danced on the houses across the street from me.

I took out the card Sebastian gave me. Randy was right, back at school, when he said that the brown lines looked like a tree. Then there were the ten green handprints. And the three little red slashes to the left of the "tree" — what were those? Was the whole thing a message? Did it have to do with "A Cleft Mind"?

If the brown lines were a tree, which one was it? There were two pine trees in the backyard of my old house. There were the tall palm trees at school.

One tree. The most important tree, at least for me, was the big pine at the park playground around the corner from my old house. The one Dad used to take me and Alyssa to. And the red marks—

The swings? Could be. Maybe he didn't want to put all four swing set poles on the card, so he put only three marks, knowing that, in my mind, I would replace the missing pole. It was just an idea, but it was the only one I had.

A cop car rolled by way too slowly. The officer looked right at me and slammed on his brakes. The squeal of the tires sounded like a dog's yelp when you accidentally step on its paw.

"Hey kid, come here," he said, motioning me over. He had a crew cut, with dark shades and the typical cop mustache.

"What do you want?" I asked, still sitting on the ground. I was nervous, but tried to calm myself. After all, there were lots of people, and lots of problems, in this neighborhood.

"I just want to talk to you," the cop said. "Come over here."

Chirps and beeps from his radio. I stood up and hobbled over to the car. The officer's window was half down.

"We're looking for a kid named Justin," he said. "You know him?"

Maybe it was another Justin. But I knew it wasn't. The blood in my head turned to ice water. Stay cool. I went into acting mode, scratching my chin like I was trying to figure out who this "Justin" kid was.

"Justin, Justin…yeah, the name sounds familiar," I told him. "I think he hangs out in this neighborhood." The officer checked his computer screen.

"We're still waiting for his description," he said. He took off his shades and folded them into his shirt pocket. "Can you tell me what this Justin kid looks like?"

"Sure," I said. "He's about… five feet nine, really buff guy. You know, lotsa muscles. Curly, longish blond hair, rides around on one of those scooters."

The cop finished scribbling in a notebook, thanked me, and drove away, his head turning left and right as he scanned the neighborhood, *looking for me*.

In less than one day, I had gone from sixth grader to outlaw. And if that cop was looking for me, the others were, too. As I limped back to the sidewalk, I caught a few scratchy words from the officer's radio:

"... approximately five foot three, black backpack, on foot. Last known location was downtown area but could be headed toward ..."

The officer jammed the car into reverse and raced back to where I was — or used to be. Swollen ankle or not, I was already halfway over the fence and heading into my neighbor's yard.

I was running from the cops.

Adrenaline surged through me. My foot didn't hurt anymore. I jumped down from the fence. My backpack snagged on a nail. In the half second it took me to unstick it, the cop was out of his car and climbing over the fence.

I made it to the next yard and shot put my backpack over the fence, scampering up and over it. If I lost that one cop, I might be able to get away. But if he called for backup, it would be over. I hoped he would try to be a hero and catch me himself.

There was one more backyard before mine. The fence was tall, and I could barely grab the top. Somehow, I pulled myself up. He was closer now. I was losing the race.

Balancing on top of the fence, I tight-roped to the roof of my neighbor's house. It was steep. I scrambled up toward the chimney, thinking I could spot an escape route from there.

I almost made it. My bare foot slipped on a loose shingle and I slid down toward the edge of the roof, grasping wildly at nothing. Only the rain gutter stopped me from going over the side. I held on to it with both hands while my body dangled over a ten-foot drop.

Gravity's victory was inevitable. My fingers were losing their grip, slowly sliding off a rusty section of rain gutter.

There were more cops now. They were talking and laughing on the grass below me. I heard a gate open and close.

"Thanks, fellas. I'll take it from here. Come here, boy." I felt a strong hand wrap around my swollen ankle and begin to pull. I couldn't hold on anymore.

"Mom!" I screamed.

"Mom!"

I fell.

CHAPTER 10:
The Punch

I opened my eyes.

I was lying on my side, looking at my backpack.

It was vibrating.

I was vibrating.

I was in the back seat of the Tank's Mercedes. My head felt like it had been hit by a truck. I didn't want him to know I was awake. I unstuck my sweaty face from the leather seat. The Tank's angry scowl was visible in the rear-view mirror.

I checked my pants for the card, but it was gone. My pockets were turned inside out. It was all right; I had memorized every detail of the card. My journal was on the floor, next to my backpack.

Still facedown, I looked out the left rear window. Power poles, trees, and billboards streamed past, all of them so familiar that I had no idea where we were.

The Tank picked up his cell from the center console. He tapped on the keypad with his thumb, glancing up at the road every couple of seconds. The thick muscles in his forearm twitched like they were excited to have something to do.

"Hey, it's me," he told someone. "Yeah, I've got him. Uh-huh. Yeah, we're already on the road. No, I didn't find anything, just some crap in his backpack." There was a pause.

"No, he's still out of it," the Tank said. "Listen, Jerry, I'm almost there. I'll go through his stuff more carefully, maybe knock some sense into him." Another pause, this one longer.

"Damn it, man, don't worry about it!" the Tank yelled. "I'll get what we need from him! What's that? Oh, his mom, right. I had her locked up. A shrink friend of mine put her on a 5150 hold — she'll be out of the picture for at least 72 hours. I can't have the boy talking to her."

"Alyssa and my son Junior are staying with a friend for a couple of days," the Tank said. "The story is that the kids' mother and I had to make an emergency trip out of town. Hold on a minute. Someone's been in back of me for a while now. Wait a second."

The Tank put the phone down and checked the rear-view mirror. Then he grabbed the wheel with both hands and swerved right, pulling on to another street. He picked up the phone again.

"O.K., false alarm," he said. "Anyway, believe me, Jerry, with the two days I'll have with the boy, I'll get him to talk. If he knows anything about that pass phrase, I'll find out. All right. O.K. Later."

I sat up and looked at him through the mirror.

"Sleep well?" he asked sarcastically.

I said nothing.

"The game's up, Justin," he said. "I'll give you credit, though — you're a smart one."

"What do you mean?"

"Figuring it out," he said, looking back at me. "Arch-Tech, C-Metal...look, I'll be honest: I didn't think you could put the pieces together like you did. But it really doesn't matter now."

"What are you talking about?" I felt like I wasn't even in the car with him, not even in my own body. The car stopped at a red light.

"Boy," he said, "there are two ways we can do this: the easy way or the hard way. Your father chose the hard way. I suggest that you don't make the same mistake."

I pretended not to listen. Traffic was a massive metal centipede, inching its way forward one cold, shiny segment at a time. A pretty woman holding a laptop computer stared down at me from a billboard. Her eyes followed mine until she disappeared.

"You know something about my dad?" I already knew the answer.

"You know what a dichotomy is?" he asked, not stopping to hear my answer. "It's when two opposite things occur at the same time. Danny Tyme was a dichotomy. He was both really stupid and incredibly smart. Stupid not to give me the pass phrase to the C-Metal file," he said. "And smart enough to layer the encryption so deeply that even my team still can't touch it."

The Tank must have thought my dad had given me or left me something, maybe a clue to the pass phrase. Suddenly, the Tank's control of the house trespassing of my room made sense. He was looking for something.

It was then that I realized he really was the evil creep I always suspected him of being. And, strangely, it freed me up to talk to him.

"What's the tattoo about?"

For a second, he seemed surprised that I knew. Then, he pulled back his sleeve and exposed the sharp greens and yellows wrapped around his massive arm. The colors seemed brighter now, the words easier to read.

"I got it in the Army."

Six words. It was the most he had ever spoken to me without sounding pissed off.

"What's that mean?" I asked. "'Smarter, Faster, Stronger, Better'."

"'94 Bravo' was the group ID for my unit," he said. "We were known as 'Black Fox'. Four soldiers. Our mission was to discover or develop materials that would save the military money. And we hit the jackpot with Danny Tyme and C-Metal."

"The four words you asked about refer to the men in our unit as well as the materials we worked with. The columns you see stand for strength; the daggers, well, you can let your imagination answer that one."

I didn't like how that sounded.

"What happened to my dad?"

"Boy, he's gone. The details are not important. Leave it alone."

Gone. What did that mean? *Gone,* as in dead? Or *gone,* as in somewhere else? I stared at the back of his big, bald head. I imagined that my hands were wrapped around his neck and I was squeezing the life out of him. I would push his lifeless body out of the car and drive away.

I didn't know that I was crying until I touched my face and felt the tears. I wiped them away. I didn't want him to think he had the power to make me cry.

He merged into a lane that led to the freeway on-ramp. I should've been looking at the signs to figure out where I was, but I didn't care.

"You probably want to know how your mom fits into this, right?" he asked, as the Mercedes accelerated on to the freeway. "I guess I can tell you now. I mean, since you're either going to disappear like your dad, or...anyway, it doesn't really matter what you know. In a couple days, I'll have the pass phrase, and I'll be gone— like Danny Tyme."

Traffic was lighter on the freeway. I looked through the back window and saw a black motorcycle about five car lengths back.

"After your dad wouldn't cooperate, I had a talk with Desiree. I explained to her how important it was that I found out where Danny had put the key to this incredible technology— the pass phrase. We had your dad's computers; that wasn't the problem. We just couldn't access what we needed. She told me she didn't know anything about it."

The Mercedes was flying down the freeway. The speedometer read 85. I looked back and the motorcycle was barely visible. I knew it was one in a million, but there was a chance.

"I told your mother that she was putting Danny in danger by not telling me what she knew, but she still wouldn't talk," he said. "Or maybe she really *didn't* know anything. That's when my focus fell on you."

"A member of Black Fox was convinced that Danny would have left you a clue. I believe you met him at Arch-Tech earlier today. His name is Jerry Smith."

"Personally, I didn't think your father would be dumb enough to trust a little boy, but I couldn't take a chance, not with something worth so much. So I made an arrangement with your mother. You were in the third grade."

"What was the arrangement?"

"I move you three into my house. Desiree keeps her mouth shut about Danny, Arch-Tech, and C-Metal. In return, you and Alyssa don't get hurt."

So my mom knew. And the Tank stopped her from telling me. And it tore her apart, threw her into a depression.

The Tank seemed almost relieved to be able to tell me everything. He wasn't paying attention to me, just talking a mile a minute. Using my good foot, I managed to scoot my journal close to me and then shuffle it into my open backpack.

"It has been hell on your mother," he said. "She couldn't stand me— still can't. But based on what happened to your dad, she knew what I was capable of."

"Of course, we never got married. That would have left a paper trail. As for Frank, Jr., well, he was an awkward but necessary step in the illusion."

Awkward but necessary? My little brother? Only the Tank, with his total lack of human emotion, would be able to label a person like that, let alone a little baby.

"Where is my mom?" I blurted.

"Don't bark at me, you little bastard," the Tank said, his voice growing colder. "I needed her out of the way for a couple of days while I dealt with you. You know, Justin, if you help me find what I need, you can all be back together again before you know it."

I didn't believe him. It was dark. We were back on city streets. It was hard to think, but one thing was crystal clear: I had to get out of the car.

The Mercedes stopped at a red light. Out the back window I saw a single headlamp. At that second, there were probably ten thousand black motorcycles on the street. But I had a feeling.

"Well, it sounds like your plan for getting rich is pretty solid," I said. "Except you forgot one important thing."

"What's that?" he asked, as the light turned green.

"Me!"

I snatched the Tank's cell phone off the console with one hand and grabbed my backpack with the other. I was out the door and running in the opposite direction at full speed.

I turned and looked back. The Tank, all 250 pounds of him, jumped out of the car and took off after me, leaving the car at the intersection. Angry drivers were yelling and honking their horns. I sprinted a hundred feet before I caught the glare of the motor-cycle headlamp. It was him!

"Get on!" Mr. Dave yelled as the helmet flew through the air at me. I slammed it on to my head, jumped on the bike, and grabbed the back of Mr. Dave's jacket while he pulled back on the accelerator. The bike growled and lurched forward.

The Tank was five or six car lengths away when he saw us. For a second, he froze, like he couldn't understand what was happening. Then, as the bike moved toward him, he bent down into a football player stance, like he was about to make a tackle. The veins swelled in his neck. This maniac was actually going to try to take us down!

But Mr. Dave was too quick for him. We picked up speed and I leaned with him as he maneuvered the bike around the Tank's right side. As we jammed past him, I reached out my hand and punched him in the face as hard as I could.

The last word I heard from him was almost lost in our exhaust as we hurtled past the Mercedes and down the street: "Justinnnn!"

I turned around and gave him my best one-fingered parade wave. He was a pathetic figure, standing in the middle of the intersection, breathing hard, hands on his knees in frustration. I almost felt sorry for him. Almost.

CHAPTER 11:
Hiding Out

It's impossible to have a conversation on a motorcycle, so I didn't try. Mr. Dave made some quick, random turns, probably to make sure that the Tank wasn't following us. We headed north, on an access road that ran parallel to the freeway.

I felt free. On the dark road, we were just a blazing shaft of light. It was cold out, but I didn't feel it. My bare feet were swollen blocks of ice.

We rode into a quiet neighborhood and turned on to a dirt road. Mr. Dave killed the headlamp but kept going. It was a beautiful night. The storm had moved on, revealing a clear, black sky. A pale white, egg-shaped moon was rising directly in front of us, lighting up the palm trees that lined the road.

Two more lefts and we pulled in to a driveway. Mr. Dave shut off the engine, and we rolled up toward a small apartment set back from the road. We stopped under a sagging cloth overhang, next to a pile of metal parts that at one time might have been a motorcycle.

The rumbling of the motorcycle's engine was etched into my brain. After I got off the bike, the silence seemed even louder. Mr. Dave gestured for me to give him the helmet. We hadn't spoken since I had jumped on the bike back at the intersection and I wondered if he was being quiet for a reason — were we not supposed to be there?

He went to the front door. I followed him. For the first time since before I ran from the cops, my ankle hurt. Not bad— just throbbed a little. Mr. Dave paused at the door and looked back out toward the street. I did too. He unlocked the door, pushed it open, and found a light switch on the wall just inside.

I knew right away that it was his place. Posters of motorcycles and muscle cars. The carpet so stained with motor oil that it was almost totally black. In one corner, a grimy lamp sat on a dusty end table, next to a framed photograph of a boy who looked about my age. He was sitting on a dirt bike, smiling.

There was a small kitchen attached to the living room, with a sink full of dishes that spilled out over the counter. If neat-freak Tank saw Mr. Dave's place he would have had a heart attack. I wished he could have seen it.

Mr. Dave threw his leather jacket on to the couch. "Sorry about the mess," he said.

"It doesn't bother me."

I couldn't believe that, after rescuing me from the Tank, Mr. Dave was apologizing for anything.

"Take a load off, little buddy," he said. "Helluva day, huh?"

I tossed my backpack on to the floor and plopped down on to the couch. It felt good to be somewhere where I could relax.

"I'm gonna grab an ice pack for your ankle," Mr. Dave said, walking into the kitchen. "Then I'll whip us up some grub and you can tell me what kind of mess you've got yourself into."

I zipped open my backpack and took out the Tank's cell phone. I thought I knew what the Tank meant, on the phone, when he said a doctor put my mom "on a hold." One of those TV docs, Dr. Fred, had talked about it on his show. A hold was when a doctor forced someone into a clinic or hospital, to be observed. With the Tank's cell, maybe I could find her. And find my brother and sister, who the Tank had said were with a friend.

The battery icon read less than a quarter, so I wouldn't have much time to use it; I didn't have a charger for it. I pressed the menu button.

"Whoa, Justin, hold up," Mr. Dave said. "Don't use that thing. The big guy might try to trace it. You better turn it off."

I hadn't thought of that. I held down the power button until the screen went black. Mr. Dave went back to the kitchen and came back with the ice pack, which he tossed underhand to me. Then he grabbed a rusty fold-up chair and stuck it under my bad ankle.

"Hold the ice on your ankle until it gets too cold," he said. "Then hold it for another five minutes. It should go pretty numb."

He returned to the kitchen and started pulling stuff out of the cupboards and the fridge, tossing them on to the only spot on the counter not covered with dirty dishes.

"How's the ice feel?" he asked.

"It's cold," I said. "I think my ankle's getting numb already."

"That's what's supposed to happen," he said, filling up a large pot with tap water. "So," he asked, "who's the big bald dude? He didn't look too happy to lose you today."

"His name is Frank," I said. "He's my step-dad. At least, I thought he was, before today."

Mr. Dave stuck the pot of water on to one of the burners. The stove was the old-fashioned gas kind; we used to have one, and I half-remembered my dad in front of it.

He cranked the dial and there was a ticking sound. He pulled a wooden match out of a box, flicked it against the bottom of his boot, and touched the match to the burner. The flames jumped to life. He threw the match in the sink, wiped his hands on a towel, and walked back over to me.

I described everything that happened to me the last three days. The journal. The business card from the box. My trip downtown. Jerry Smith and Arch-Tech. My meeting with Sebastian and the card he gave me that matched my art project. C-Metal. The sticky note at Skippy's. That phrase, "A Cleft Mind."

While I talked, Mr. Dave went back and forth to the kitchen. He stirred the pasta, buttered the bread, and poured the drinks.

I left out the part about how my dad's card reminded me of the park near my old house. If the Tank ever caught up with Mr. Dave, I didn't want him to know anything that might put him in danger. The Tank couldn't make Mr. Dave tell him something he didn't know.

Mr. Dave leaned back in his chair and ran his hand through his beard a few times, like he was thinking. I expected questions. But there weren't any.

"And I thought *I* had a tough day," he said. "You must be starving. Let's eat."

We sat at the small table in the corner of the kitchen. It felt like I hadn't eaten in days. The last thing I had was that pathetic snack at the restaurant.

The meal Mr. Dave prepared looked delicious: A huge pile of

steaming-hot spaghetti, topped with an avalanche of meaty red sauce that dripped down like molten lava; a plate of thick, buttery garlic bread; a big slice of cherry pie buried under a landslide of vanilla ice cream; and a tall glass of milk.

Neither of us said a word; we just ate. The pasta was perfect, and the garlic bread was the best I've ever had. The cherry pie and ice cream were awesome.

After ten minutes, I sat back from the table. Mr. Dave let out a loud burp and I laughed. It had been a couple days since I had laughed.

"How was dinner?" he asked.

"Great. I can't move. I'm stuffed."

"How's the foot?"

"It's better," I said, giving it a quick look. "The swelling's down, and it doesn't hurt, not now anyway."

"Give me the ice pack," he told me, getting up from the table. "I'll stick it back into the freezer for later."

Mr. Dave pulled out a cigar from a brown wooden box ("It's called a stogie," he said) and lit it up, puffing until the tip glowed cherry-red.

He tilted his head back and blew a smoke ring toward the light fixture above us, a perfect, donut-shaped circle that kept its form until it dissolved into a smoky grey cloud that hung over the kitchen.

"So, Justin, this Frank dude sounds like a real bad hombre," Mr. Dave said.

"He is."

"Where do you think he might have put your sister and brother?"

"He said they were with a friend," I said. "But I don't know."

"And you think he might have used his cell to make the arrangements?" he asked.

"I hope so," I told him. "Right now, it's all I got. But the battery is low. I won't have much time with it on before it dies."

"Let me see it real quick," he said. "I might have a charger for it around this dump somewhere."

I tossed him the phone and he disappeared down the hall, returning a minute later with a greasy denim bag. He unzipped it and searched around inside.

"Ah-hah!" he said triumphantly. "I knew I had the right one somewhere."

He plugged the charger into an outlet in the kitchen and then attached it to the Tank's cell phone.

"Charge it overnight," he said. "That'll be plenty of juice for it. In the morning, you can turn it on for a minute or two, but only to check his outgoing calls. If you need to *make* any calls, use my cell. It's in the kitchen."

"Thanks, Mr. Dave," I said. "Hey, can I ask you something?"

"That was something already," he said, smiling. "Kidding. Fire away."

"What happened after you dropped me off?" I asked. "I mean, how did you end up following us?"

"My gut feeling was to stick around," he said. "You seemed pretty stressed out when I dropped you off. Plus, the place was crawling with police. So I rode to the end of the block and watched it go down from there."

"What did you see?"

"From where I was, not a lot," he said. "A crap load of cops took off running toward this one house. Then, the Mercedes pulled up and the big guy got out. "

"Next thing I saw, he was carrying you over his shoulder. You were out cold. He stuck you in the back seat. I let him get a couple blocks away before I started to follow."

"What was your plan?" I asked. "Did you have one?"

"Nope," he said. "All I knew was that my little buddy was in trouble. And it was way more serious than just a sprained ankle. I'm just glad I was there."

"Me, too."

I looked over at the photograph of the boy.

"Can I ask you something else?"

"You want to know who he is?"

"Yeah."

Mr. Dave got up and walked over to the table. He picked up the photo and wiped some dust off of it with his hand. He looked at it and put it back down.

"That's my son, DeShawn," he said. "He — passed away."

His words were empty, like all the emotion of that terrible loss had already drained out of him.

"You know, Justin," he said, "you remind me of DeShawn. You're curious, like he was. And smart."

I looked at the picture again. In the boy's eyes, I could see a hint of his father, and his smile made me think of Mr. Dave flirting with the cafeteria ladies. I wanted to know how DeShawn died, but I couldn't think of a polite way to ask. And Mr. Dave didn't volunteer the information. So we left it at that.

"Listen, Justin," he said, standing up and stretching, "I'm beat. I'm gonna hit the sack. There's a towel in the bathroom for you if you want to clean up. Help yourself to anything in the fridge. And don't forget the ice."

Mr. Dave walked over to the front door and turned the deadbolt counter clock-wise. Then he chained the top lock and tested the door by pulling and pushing on the handle a few times.

"I hope the couch is OK for you," he said. "I'll keep the heater on, but in case you get cold, there are blankets in the closet. Oh, and before I forget, you might want to have something to put on your feet in the morning." He went to the closet and tossed out a pair of dirty white tennis shoes.

"Those should do," he said. "They were DeShawn's. You look about his size. If they don't work, there are more in there. Anything else you need?"

"Would you happen to have a computer here, with Internet access?" I asked.

"Yeah, there's a beat-up old laptop in the drawer," he said, pointing to the table that had DeShawn's picture on it. "The signal is weak and pretty spotty, but it's free. I steal it from my neighbor."

"Thanks, Mr. Dave," I said. "For everything."

"You got it, little buddy. Good night."

"Night." He gave me the thumbs-up sign, and walked down the hallway. I heard a door close.

I pulled the laptop out of the drawer, opened it up, turned it on, and put it down at the kitchen table. Battery read 63%. Signal strength was only one out of four bars, but it looked stable. I found the built-in dictionary application and typed:

A Cleft Mind

It came back:

No results found.

I cleared it and entered just one of the words:

Cleft

It came back:

"Adjective: Split or divided."

Split or divided. Didn't help.

I thought about putting the phrase into a search engine. But if "A Cleft Mind" really was a message to me, my dad must have known that there was a chance the Tank would read the cover of the journal. Why would he leave a clue online? Too obvious. What the heck; I tried it anyway.

I opened up the browser:

Cannot connect to Internet. Please check your connection and try again.

Signal strength was zero.

Mr. Dave told me that he was using a neighbor's signal. Either the neighbor had shut it off, or the signal was so weak that the laptop couldn't pick it up. Either way, I was out of luck. I closed the computer and put it back in the drawer.

On the kitchen table were a few 3x5 note cards. I wrote the letters of "A Cleft Mind" on one of the cards, spaced randomly, in no particular order:

$$f \quad C \quad e \quad A \quad i \quad M \quad d \quad n \quad l \quad t$$

I looked at the note card. Somewhere in there was a message. Maybe I had been too focused on that phrase. Maybe it had more to do with the letters themselves.

I ripped the card into ten pieces, with one letter on each piece. Then I spread them around the table in front of me. By moving the letters around, I could spell different words.

Clam Fend It.

No.

Calf Mid Net.

I don't think so.

Maced Flint?

Nope.

Ad Cent Film.

Not even close.

Find Cat Elm.

No, but I kept *Find* off to the side.

Find Mac Let.

Nope.

Find At Elmc.

Not even.

Find C Metal.

Holy crap.

No. No way. Couldn't be. Too easy.

Find C Metal.

That's what my dad was trying to tell me. Three years ago, when he made sure that the journal would get to the right kid. Three years ago, when he wrote "A Cleft Mind" on the card for Sebastian.

Find C-Metal.

OK, Dad, I got your message. *Find C-Metal.* But how? Where? What was I supposed to do? I had nothing.

I sat at the table, holding the bits of shredded card. There was nothing more I could do that day. I missed my family. I was tired. Really tired.

CHAPTER 12:
The Shed

I was alone in the back row of a dark movie theater. I didn't know how I had gotten there. There was someone sitting in the middle of the front row.

"Excuse me!" I said loudly.

The person didn't move.

"Hello!" I tried again.

The figure stood up and turned around. It was my dad!

"Dad!" I yelled. All the weight suddenly lifted off of me. I was light. I ran to the aisle, my feet barely touching the floor, and raced down to the front row.

I was ten feet from him when I looked up. It wasn't my dad anymore.

"Come here, boy."

I woke up, drenched in sweat. It was morning. I lay there and let my heartbeat slow down. I hadn't moved all night. One of those coma-sleeps. The icepack was on the carpet next to the couch. There was a note on top of my backpack.

Hey little buddy,

I had to roll out of here early today. You looked like you needed the rest so I didn't wake you. I know with everything you've got going on that you probably won't be going to school today. Don't spend too much time with the big guy's cell phone on. Remember to use my cell to make any calls. Help yourself to breakfast; there's cereal, toast, whatever you can find. In the kitchen drawer by the fridge I left you an envelope – it might come in handy. Be careful today.

Mr. Dave

I poured a bowl of cereal and turned on the little black and white TV in the living room. I hadn't even noticed it the night before, it was so small. There was no remote; I pulled a little knob to turn it on, and changed the dial manually to get channels. Mr. Dave's old school technology. Only one channel came in clear. Ronny Rectangle was on. But it didn't feel right watching it without my little brother.

I sat down at the kitchen table. I was nervous about turning on the Tank's cell phone. What Mr. Dave had said, about the Tank tracking my location, gave me the chills.

The fastest way of checking call history would be to write all the numbers down at once, and then turn off the phone. After that, I was going to break the phone, smash it. Once the screen lit up, I pushed the menu button, went to 'call history', and wrote down the first ten phone numbers I saw, five from 'dialed' and five from 'received'. Then I held the power button down. I dug through a couple of kitchen drawers until I found my weapon — a hammer. The back door to the house opened up to a small, fenced-in yard that had a metal shed in one corner.

I put the phone down on the paved path that ran from the back door to the shed. I got on my knees, warmed up with a couple slow-motion practice swings, and then smashed the hammer down. It smacked the cement, sparked, and bounced back up at me.

My second try was a direct hit. The phone exploded into a hundred shards of metal and plastic. I worked it over a few more times to make sure there was no way it could ever give off a signal again. Then I went to the shed to check for a broom.

There was a lock, but it wasn't pressed closed. I pulled it from the latch and slid the metal doors open. Inside, it was dark and dusty. A musty odor hung in the air. The broom and dustpan were in the corner.

A black metallic bookshelf leaned against the back wall. I didn't want to snoop, but I was curious. There was a skateboard, a deflated basketball, two football helmets, some comic books, broken sunglasses, motocross kneepads and elbow pads and a sweatshirt. It had to be DeShawn's stuff. There was also a black plastic 8-ball, the kind you ask a question of and then shake it and read the answer.

Are my sister and brother OK?

I shook it.

Ask again later, it told me.

Will I see my dad again?

Outlook not so good.

A cigar box was on the bottom shelf. I picked it up and blew the dust off of it. I thought for a second about putting it back down, but I opened it instead. Inside, there was a mood ring that had gone black. There was also a folded-up newspaper clipping. I moved closer to the entrance so I could use the light to read it.

Fundraiser for Sick Youth Nets Little

Leaders of a school fundraiser organized to help a popular Benjamin Harrison Elementary School student cover medical treatment stemming from a rare type of cancer are disappointed with the results, but vow to continue their efforts.

Last March, DeShawn Martino, a third grader whose hobbies include football and motocross, began complaining of headaches. His father brought him to a doctor for what he thought would be a routine examination. Instead, DeShawn was diagnosed with a rare form of brain cancer.

"I expected to hear that he might be suffering from migraines, something like that," said David Martino, DeShawn's father. "Instead, it was like a bomb was dropped on us. I still can't believe he has cancer. My boy is everything to me. He's my life."

The cost of DeShawn's medical treatment quickly ran into the thousands of dollars, but Mr. Martino was comforted by the fact that his insurance was slated to cover eighty percent of any expenses incurred. Then a second bombshell: a glitch in the school district's computer had inadvertently kicked Mr. Martino and DeShawn out of the system. While the problem was being corrected, personnel at the district's Human Resources Department discovered that, during the previous year, Mr. Martino had neglected to complete paperwork critical to the continuation of his insurance coverage.

Despite Mr. Martino's pleas, his insurance company refused to cover the cost of DeShawn's treatment.

After a protracted legal battle, during which De-Shawn's condition worsened steadily, a judge sided with the insurance company, ruling that the decision to refuse coverage had precedent and thus was legal.

Mr. Martino was left unable to cover his son's rising medical bills. Yesterday's fundraiser, attended by Ben Harrison staff, students, and families, raised $8,000 for DeShawn's treatment, only a fraction of what was needed.

Despite the difficult circumstances, Mr. Martino is trying to stay upbeat. "I need to be positive for De-Shawn," he said, showing off a photo of his son on a motorcycle. "He's counting on me. We'll find the money, somehow."

I learned more about Mr. Dave from that article than from all the times I had visited him in his office. I knew I should have put the article back in the box, but I didn't. I folded it up and put it in my pocket. I don't know why, but it felt important enough for me to keep.

I swept up the broken bits of the phone and dumped them in a trashcan behind the shed. Then I returned the broom and dustpan and slid the doors closed, arranging the lock like I had found it.

It was time to make some calls and try to find out where the Tank had put my family. I recognized only two of the numbers: the Tank's house, and the phone number to Benjamin Harrison Elementary. Some of the other numbers had different area codes.

Maybe the Tank knew I would call and he set some kind of trap for me. Could he have known I'd steal his phone? Is that why he put it on the center console, easily within my reach? But if that was true, he would have had to know that I would jump out. And *I* didn't even know I would do that until a minute before I jumped. No, he couldn't be *that* good. He couldn't have known I would take his phone.

I didn't know what I was going to say. I dialed the first number on the list. It rang twice. Three times. Four. Next number. One ring, and then a recording:

"You've reached Lieutenant Colonel Richard Masterson. At the tone, please leave a mes—"

I hit the 'end' key. Military. No surprise there.

Next number. One ring. Another. A third.

"Hello?" It was a male voice, one I didn't recognize.

"Hello?" he said. "Anyone there?"

"Yes, uh—"

"Justin? Is that you?" It was more whisper than voice.

"Who is this?" I asked.

"I'm glad you found us," he said. "But we can't talk on the phone."

"Tell me who you are or this conversation is over."

"I can't, not right now," he said. "You'll just have to trust me."

"It's hard to trust anybody," I said, my adrenalin rising. "This number was in Frank's phone. Why should I believe anything you tell me?"

"OK, don't trust me then," he said. "But would it hurt to listen, at least? I'm going to give you an address. Ronny, Sally, and Tony are there. Get there as soon as you can. Got a pen?"

I thought about hanging up. But instead I picked up a pen.

"OK, go ahead."

"5503 Jade Court. It's the smallest place on the block."

I struggled to write down the address while holding the cell phone between my shoulder and ear. As I finished writing the last two letters of "Court," the phone slipped and fell on to the table, bounced once, and hit the floor. I picked it up quickly.

"Is that it?" I asked.

No response.

"Hello?"

He was gone.

I wondered how the man on the phone recognized my voice. And who were Ronny, Sally and Tony?

Ronny, Sally, and Tony. Those names sounded familiar…and then, there it was, the voice from TV, obnoxious and loud:

"LADIES AND GENTLEMEN, BOYS AND GIRLS, ALIENS AND EARTHLINGS, IT'S TIME FOR EVERYBODY'S FAVORITE HALF-HOUR OF TELEVISION! BUCKLE YOUR SEAT BELTS, STOW AWAY YOUR TRAY TABLES, PUT YOUR BRAINS IN THE UPRIGHT POSITION, AND GET READY TO CRASH LAND WITH THE MOST LOVABLE GROUP OF GEOMETRIC FIGURES THE UNIVERSE HAS EVER KNOWN! IT'S… RONNY RECTANGLE AND THE SUPER-SHAPES!"

That must have meant that he had Junior and Alyssa! The phone call had pumped me full of new energy. The possibility that it might be one of the Tank's tricks entered my mind, but I quickly brushed it aside.

I thought about calling more numbers to try and find my mom, but decided against it. I wanted to see how things worked out at the address the man had given me. I grabbed a phone book from on top of Mr. Dave's fridge and found the map section. The man didn't give me a city to go by, so I searched the street list for Jade Court.

Jade was at the northern most point in the city. A long bus ride, and that would cost money. Not good. I sketched a quick diagram of the streets Jade Court was close to.

I stuffed the phone numbers, the address, the map sketch, and DeShawn's newspaper article into one of the shoes Mr. Dave gave me. I put them on. They felt OK. There was a plastic shopping bag under the sink; I put my journal inside of it. Picking up the journal reminded me of my promise. It had already been four days since I had the journal and I still hadn't written a word.

I was about to leave when I remembered Mr. Dave's envelope. I grabbed it and stuck it in my pocket. I took one more look around the living room to make sure I hadn't forgotten anything. Locking the door behind me, I stepped out into a bright, cool morning.

On a normal day, I would have been at school. But that morning was far from normal. Traffic ground along a distant boulevard, maybe six long blocks away. I started off in that direction.

Curiosity got the best of me and I ripped open the envelope. Five 20-dollar bills. My money problem was solved. I knew I had to pay it back. There was a Quickie-Gas-Mart on the corner.

I bought a soda, chips, and a spicy beef jerky, and asked for three dollars in quarters with my change.

The coins jingled in my pocket as I dashed across the busy boulevard to the bus stop. Someone told me once that if you're farther than a hundred feet away from a traffic signal, it isn't against the law. I wondered if that would work with the cops. But I guessed that, if the Tank still had the cops looking for me, a jaywalking ticket would be the least of my problems.

The sign at the bus stop had both Route 65 and 14. I took out the map sketch. Both the routes went there. I decided to take whichever came first.

65 rolled up and I jumped aboard, bought a day pass, and walked to the back. I sat down in the middle, with the rear emergency exit window directly behind me. You never know.

The ride took about a half-hour. I got off a stop early, just in case. Things had been unpredictable lately, and I wasn't going to take any chances.

No one was around. Houses sat quietly, next to each other, obedient wooden pets waiting patiently for their owners' return. Jade was one block up. I wrapped the handle of the plastic bag tightly around my wrist in case I had to run.

I got to the corner of Jade and Garvey. Jade ended at Garvey, so to be on it, I could only make a left. There was a liquor store on the corner. The address "5508" was hand-painted in crooked red letters on the wall next to the entrance. There was a phone booth on the side of the small parking lot.

5503 Jade Court. It's the smallest place on the block. I had to be close. I walked past the liquor store, checking behind me to see if any cars were coming.

The first house on the left was a small blue A-frame with dark brown shutters, a security screen door, and a lawn in desperate need of mowing. There was a green sedan parked in the driveway, but judging by the weeds growing from under it, it hadn't moved for a while.

I saw the first two letters of the address, "55," but the rest was hidden behind a plant. I moved a few steps to each side, trying to get a glimpse of the other two numbers, but no luck. I had to move the plant. I walked up to the house, listening for any noises. Nothing.

I made it to the front door, and I didn't have to move the plant after all. I saw all four numbers: 5500.

I walked back to the sidewalk. I had to have gone too far. The liquor store was 5508. 5503 should have been in between those two numbers. Maybe it was on the other side of the street. But from where I stood, I could see three addresses in a row on that side: 5531, 5537, and 5541.

Something wasn't right. I went back to the liquor store to double-check that address. 5508.

It's the smallest place on the block.

I looked at the phone booth. It was scratched up badly, plastered with graffiti, and had survived at least one collision with a car. I pulled open the folding door and went inside. I picked up the receiver and put it to my ear. Dial tone. I hung up. The empty plastic phone book cover swung limply.

I stuck a finger in the coin return slot. I felt something, and pulled it out. A piece of paper, tightly folded:

Go back to Garvey and make a right.
Go to Strings Central.
Ask for Dutch.

It had to be for me. I went back to the corner, turned right, and started walking, checking both sides of the street for something called Strings Central. What kind of business could survive selling string?

After three very long blocks, I saw a sign on a two-story brick building on my side of the street. Next to the words "Strings Central," there was a green guitar, neon flickering on and off.

It was a big place. Guitars of every color, size, and shape hung from hooks on the walls. Huge posters of rock stars and rock bands loomed over me. Rows of guitar strings, amps, and songbooks lined the floor.

A man with a razor-sharp purple mohawk sat on a stool with his eyes closed, twanging an out-of-tune acoustic guitar. The employee standing next to him grimaced. I recognized Mohawk Man's song from Mr. Dave's office.

A lady with choppy hair, black leather pants and a ripped white tank top stood behind the register, wrapping stacks of dollar bills with rubber bands. She looked up at me but continued to count, mouthing the numbers silently.

"How can I help you?" she asked.

"Is Dutch here?"

The lady stopped counting, put the cash back in the register, and closed the drawer a little too hard.

"Stay here," she ordered me.

She walked to the back of the store. A second later, I saw her profile through a window of a back room. She spoke to someone I couldn't see.

The lady returned, except this time on my side of the counter.

"Walk through the store and out the back," she said quietly. "Dutch is waiting for you in a car."

A thousand doubts filled my head. I was about to walk into a completely unknown situation, leaving myself vulnerable to anything.

"What are you waiting for?" the lady asked in a slightly annoyed tone of voice.

I couldn't answer her.

"Hey, don't worry," she said, trying to comfort me. "I know him. Just go." Something in the lady's eyes told me that it wasn't the Tank or one of his cops out there, waiting for me. I walked to the back, and out the door.

CHAPTER 13:
The Finger

I stood in the back parking lot of Strings Central. The door closed behind me. A black four-door sedan with tinted windows was idling in front of me.

I didn't move. Neither did the car. I thought about running. The driver's window rolled down a few inches. An index finger appeared from above the window, slowly beckoning me over. It looked too skinny to be the Tank's finger.

Reluctantly, I walked toward the car. The finger gestured for me to go to the passenger side. I wanted to see into the car, but I followed the finger's directions. I walked to the passenger door. It was open a crack.

"It's all right, Justin. You can trust me."

It was the voice from the phone. I climbed in and pulled the door closed. Before I had a chance to put on my seat belt, the car was moving. We left the parking lot, turned right onto Garvey and sped away.

The driver looked about forty, with a five o'clock shadow and salty grey hair. He had on slacks and a brown sports jacket.

"Sorry about the cat-and-mouse game," he said. "I had to make sure you weren't being followed."

"Are you Dutch?" I asked him.

"What? Oh, no. That's just the name I gave my friend at the music store for when you showed up— if you showed up."

"So, who are you?"

"I'm Darren Hooper."

"Who?"

"Your teacher's husband."

It didn't register. I understood the words, but together they didn't make sense.

"I know you must be confused with everything that's been happening, Justin," he said. "I hope I can help you sort some of it out."

"Where are my brother and sister?" I asked impatiently. "And my mom?"

"They're all fine," he said. Something in his voice made me want to believe him. "Frank, Jr. and Alyssa are safe. They're with my wife at our house. We're on the way to meet up with them right now."

"What about my mom?"

He waited before answering.

"She's safe as well," he said, hesitantly. "Your mom is getting some help. She's in a clinic. Here in town." There was something like regret in his voice.

"Is it a mental hospital?" I asked.

"I guess you could call it that," he said.

An image came to mind: my mom in a bathrobe and slippers, head down and shoulders slumped, shuffling down a long hallway. I should have been elated that Mr. Hooper had found me, and that I would be reunited with my brother and sister. But the thought of my mom being locked up made me anxious.

"But, Justin, the important thing is that you and your family are OK."

It was quiet for a minute. I looked out the window. Auto-dealerships. Shiny new cars sat in perfect rows, like vegetables in a field, waiting to be picked.

"So, you worked with my dad?"

"Yes I did," he said. "Unfortunately, none of his architectural genius rubbed off on me." He laughed nervously.

"There were four of us," Mr. Hooper continued. "Jerry Smith, who was the group leader, myself, your father, and a man named Sebastian Seely."

"I know Sebastian," I told him. "I met him at Arch-Tech. Or, he met me, I guess. And I also talked to Mr. Smith. He lied right to my face, told me he had never heard of Danny Tyme."

"Mrs. Hooper told me that your stepfather, Frank, came to Ben Harrison yesterday after the attendance secretary called about your absence," Mr. Hooper said. "Someone at Arch-Tech may have told him that you had been there, asking questions."

Jerry Smith. Had to be.

"Frank came to my wife's classroom and made an unusual

request," he said. "He told her that your mom was in crisis, some sort of nervous condition, and that he needed our help with Alyssa and Frank, Jr. for a couple of days."

"In reality, though, I think that Frank just wanted to find you, and make sure he had no distractions once he did," Mr. Hooper said. "Your step-dad must think you have something that he really wants. Are you aware of the project our group was working on?"

"Yeah, Sebastian told me about C-Metal," I said. "But I still don't really understand it."

"Did Sebastian mention to you how much the technology is worth?"

"Yeah, he said a whole lot."

"Billions of dollars, Justin," he said. "*Billions.* That much money does strange things to people. Jerry Smith used to be a good man. But after he realized how much money he could make, he changed. And whoever he was dealing with really wanted to get their hands on that stuff. I'm starting to think that Frank is involved pretty deep."

"I know he is," I said.

I had only known Mr. Hooper a few minutes, but I was comfortable with him. Still, I didn't want to tell Mr. Hooper what Sebastian had given me: the card and the message.

"Did I get Sebastian in trouble?" I asked. "Did Jerry Smith find out that we met?" Mr. Hooper didn't respond. He tightened his grip on the steering wheel and fidgeted, adjusting his side mirror.

"I wasn't going to tell you about Sebastian," he said.

"Tell me what?"

"There's something that — listen, this is hard."

"Tell me."

"Sebastian is dead. He died in a car crash, yesterday."

"No. That's not right. It can't be," I blurted, looking at Mr. Hooper to see if it was some kind of sick joke. "I just saw him." It felt like we were acting in a movie; he says something, then it was my turn. Scripted.

"It was a single-car accident," Mr. Hooper said. "The police found no sign of foul play. He was on the way home from work. His car hit a guardrail, spun around, and flipped. Sebastian was ejected from the vehicle."

"What's 'foul play'?"

"It means that the cops at the scene have already decided that it was just an accident," he said. "The case is closed."

"Is that normal?" I asked. "I mean, for the cops to finish their investigation in one day?"

"I'm not sure. I called the police department and was able to find out the name of the officer of record, but nothing else."

"Do you have the cop's name?"

"I wrote it down. Open the glove compartment for me."

I did, and Mr. Hooper leaned over and pulled a napkin out of it. He slammed the compartment shut, never taking his eyes off the road.

"Here," he said, handing it to me. "It's yours."

On the napkin was written: *Ortega, Badge 4736.* I opened my plastic bag and dropped it in.

"Now this is the hard part," Mr. Hooper said. "I believe that you and your brother and sister are in danger," he said. "And that means my wife and I, because we're helping you, are also in danger." He made a right turn and slowed down.

"I spoke with your mom this morning," he said. "I asked her permission to take you, Alyssa, and Frank, Jr. with me and my wife somewhere, kind of like — on a long trip. That was, if I was able to find you. And she gave me permission."

"A trip? Where?" I asked.

"We need to get as far away from your step-father as we can," he told me, pulling over to the curb. He turned off the ignition and unclipped his seat belt.

"I know it's sudden," he said, turning to look at me. "Believe me, it's not something we want to do right now. You and your sister should be in school. Junior should be with his mom. And Mrs. Hooper and I are leaving jobs, and lives, that we love."

I could already see the looks of surprise on the faces of my friends when a substitute teacher showed up. And I didn't. To-morrow. And the next day. And the next. Mike. Loop. Bicsan. The twins.

I felt like I had to take control of the conversation; things were moving too fast. "OK, now, hold on a second," I said to Mr. Hooper. "How do you know what Frank might do? As far as we know, he's never really hurt anyone. It's all — what do you call it? Circumstantial, that's it. Maybe we're overreacting."

"No," he said. "We're not overreacting. I know what he's capable of."

"You know? You saw him do something?"

"I've seen enough."

He unbuttoned the right cuff of his shirt and began to roll up his sleeve, slowly folding each section back. Green. Yellow. Black.

"Have you seen this before?" he asked.

I had seen it. 94 Bravo. Mr. Hooper had been Black Fox. With the Tank.

"Is that why Frank asked Mrs. Hooper to watch Alyssa and Junior?" I asked him. "Because he already knew you, from the military?"

"Yes, we were close once," he said, some sadness in his voice. "At one point, I even considered him a friend. But that was before C-Metal."

It was a lot of information in a short amount of time. So much had happened when I was younger, even before I was born.

"C'mon," Mr. Hooper said, "Let's go see your brother and sister."

"Wait. They're here?"

"Yep, two houses down." He pointed up the street. "You see the van?"

CHAPTER 14:
The Hug

We walked up to the front door of a two-story green and white Victorian. The door swung open. Alyssa was standing there.

"Justin!" She ran forward and jumped into my arms. I closed my eyes and held her. My lungs were tight with emotion.

"We're going on a trip with your teacher!" she blurted out, with the bubbly innocence of a kid who didn't know the whole story. Which, for her, was the way I wanted it, at least for a while.

"I know, Lissy, I know," I said, trying to sound happy. Through the doorway, I could see Frank, Jr. on the living room floor, playing with blocks. Next to him was a Ronny Rectangle suitcase and another bag. The Tank must have packed them.

Junior looked up at me and made his funny monkey sounds and smiled his gummy smile. I walked over to him and picked him up and hugged him. His fuzzy Ronny Rectangle pajamas were soft against me. He still had the baby-smell. I missed it.

"Are you OK, little man?" I asked.

He grabbed my nose and twisted. I took it as a "yes."

Then you appeared at the bottom of the stairs, carrying a duffel bag in each hand. You had on jeans and a long-sleeved shirt. I had never seen you dressed so casually. Your straight brown hair fell down over your shoulders.

"Hi, Justin."

"Hi."

"Did you remember?" you asked.

"Remember what?"

"To write."

I held up the plastic bag with my journal inside. "I remembered my promise," I said. "I thought about it every day. It's been a really crazy couple of days. I have plenty to put in there once I start."

"Good," you said. "Can I read it when you're done?"

"Sure."

You grabbed the bags, smiled faintly at me, and walked out the door toward the van. You tried hard not to look stressed out, but I knew you were.

"Justin, we need to get going," Mr. Hooper said to me.

"I know," I said. "But I have two stops that I need to make before we leave."

Mr. Hooper looked worried. He gestured for me to follow him into the kitchen. We sat down at the table. He spoke quietly.

"What are the stops?" he asked. "We really have to get out of here."

"First I want to see my mom," I told him. "Just to make sure she's OK."

"Justin," he said, "believe me, I understand. But you have to trust me on this one. That's the first place that your step-dad—"

"He's not my step-dad," I interrupted.

"What?"

"He never married my mom."

"I'm sorry, I didn't realize..." His voice trailed off.

"That's okay. I just found out. But don't tell my sister. She wouldn't understand."

"Of course not."

The blocks knocked against each other in the living room. Alyssa talked to Junior in a silly voice. He giggled. She was so good with her little brother.

"Anyway," Mr. Hooper continued, "Your mom's clinic is the first place that he will go to find you."

"Can I at least call her?" I asked.

"Even that's dangerous," he said. "But I guess that, if we leave the house right afterward, it would be OK. I'll make sure we have everything packed up in the van. You can take the phone into the back bedroom for privacy."

"I need the number."

Mr. Hooper walked over to the cupboard above the fridge and pulled a phone book from it.

"It's called South Bay Psychiatric Services," he said, handing me the heavy book. "Most of these places have a policy that— anyway, you can try. Make it as short a conversation as you can, all right? Once we've relocated, you can spend more time talking to her."

"I'll make it quick."

"What was your second stop?" he asked.

"It's a park." Before he spoke, I tried to explain.

"Mr. Hooper, you've asked me to trust you so far, and I have," I said. "Now, I'm asking you to trust me. This is really important. It's over by my old house. I don't think the Tank— I mean, *Frank*, has any reason to suspect that I would go there."

"You absolutely *have* to go?"

"Yes, I do. And I have cab fare if you can't give me a ride."

"Well, I guess I can drive you over there real quick while Mrs. Hooper waits here with the kids," he said. "I bought one of those throw-away pre-paid cell phones; you can use it to call your mom from the road. Sound OK?"

"Yeah."

"OK," he said. "Let's go."

We walked back to the living room. I sat down on the floor with my brother and sister. "Whatcha guys playing?" I asked.

"I'm trying to build a house," Alyssa complained in her fake sad voice, "but Junior keeps wrecking it." She leered at her little brother.

"Sis, I'm going to take a drive with Mr. Hooper. You and Junior will wait here."

"Stay here with your teacher?" she asked me, still excited from the newness of everything.

"Yes, with my teacher."

"Will you be back?"

"I'll see you soon, I promise."

She turned back to the blocks for a second, stacking a few before Junior's fist demolished her pile. She didn't seem to mind.

"Justin," she asked without looking up at me. "Do you know where we're going?"

"I think it's a surprise," I told her. Technically, it wasn't a lie.

"When will we see Mommy?"

"Lissy, Mommy is having a hard time right now. You've seen her sad before, right?"

"Yeah," she answered.

"Well, she's spending some time with people who are cheering her up."

"How long until she's happy?"

"I'm not sure," I say. "But I do know that she loves you very, very much. Don't worry about her, OK? She'll be fine, and you'll be with her soon. Now, can I ask you a favor?"

"What is it?"

141

"Promise me that, while I'm gone with Mr. Hooper, you'll be a good big sister, and listen to Mrs. Hooper. Can you do that for me?"

"Yeah."

"Gimme a hug."

She shuffled over on her knees and gave me a tight squeeze. Junior snuck up from behind, jumped onto my back, and pulled my hair. That boy is a ninja.

"Justin, we better get going." Mr. Hooper was standing in the doorway, keys in hand. Then you walked in from the kitchen.

"See you soon?" you asked me.

"Yeah," I said. "See you soon."

CHAPTER 15:
The Park

The drive back to my old neighborhood was a quiet one. Once in a while I told Mr. Hooper where to turn. I figured he had a lot to think about and would appreciate the silence.

He offered me the cell phone, but I politely said no, telling him I'd call later. I did want to call her right then, though. But I needed privacy.

The park was ahead. Nothing much had changed. A basket-ball court must have been put in a couple of years ago. A lady was walking her dog. Two guys tossed a Frisbee around.

"Can you pull over here?" I asked.

Mr. Hooper swung the car to the curb and I grabbed the door handle.

"Wait," he said, touching my arm. "How long will you be?"

"Maybe twenty minutes."

"I need to find a post office before we leave," he said. "Meet you right here in a half-hour?"

"Sounds good."

"Here's the number to the cell phone in case you need it." He handed me a slip of paper, which I added to my collection inside the plastic bag.

I stepped out and slammed the door shut. "Thanks Mr. Hooper," I said through the open window. "I appreciate the ride."

"Be careful, Justin."

He put the car back in gear and pulled away from the curb, swung a u-turn, and disappeared around the corner. I walked across the grass toward the playground.

It smelled like recess. The Frisbee players packed it in and walked past me to their car. The dog walker was gone as well. The park was empty. It was getting colder. I reached the edge of the playground. Swings. Monkey bars. Merry-go-round.

I made it to the tree. It was thicker than I remembered, and the roots had grown up and out of the ground, but it was the one on the card. I was sure of it. My dad's tree. I closed my eyes and ran my hand over its rough skin, listening for my dad's laughter.

Ten hands.

I got down on all fours. I thought about how weird it would look if anyone was watching. I put my right hand down at the base of the tree closest to the swings, on top of a thick brown root, and counted:

One.

I placed the palm of my left hand down so that it touched the end of the middle finger of my right hand.

Two.

My left hand was touching the grass.

Three.

I was moving closer to the path that bordered the sand.

Four.

Almost to the path.

Five.

I was on the path. The path may not have existed when my dad hid whatever it is that I was looking for. If he hid something. And, if he hid it there.

Six.

Closer to the sand.

Seven.

Almost to the sand.

Eight.

At the sand.

Would my dad have buried the key to a priceless technology in the sand that a hundred kids played in every day? Yeah. He might have.

Nine.

"Looking for something?"

A bolt of fear coursed through me as I looked up and squinted into the sun. A lady in an orange jumpsuit was looking down at me. She had on a cap with the city logo on it and was holding a trash poker. Parked across from her, near the bathrooms, was a small white city pickup truck.

"Uh, yeah, I lost my house key."

"Wow, that's rough," she said. "Well, if it doesn't turn up, you can contact the city's lost and found. There's always a chance someone will turn it in."

"OK, thanks."

I sensed an opportunity and went with it.

"I just wish I had something to dig with," I said. "It sure would be quicker that way. Do you have anything I can use?"

"Well, I'm not supposed to do this, but I guess it can't hurt," she said. "I found some sand toys here earlier and stuck 'em in the truck. I'll grab you one of the shovels. Just leave it in the sand when you're done."

I followed her to the truck. She opened up the tailgate and pulled out a small red plastic shovel.

"Here you go," she said, handing it to me. "Leave it in the sand, OK?"

"Will do."

The park worker slammed the tailgate closed, climbed into the truck, and drove slowly away, in the direction of the basketball courts.

Ten.

I pushed the shovel into the sand. The top layer was loose

and light and mixed with brittle pine needles and tanbark. Digging was easy. I didn't know what I was looking for so I didn't want to jam the shovel down too hard — I didn't want to break whatever it is I was supposed to find — if there was anything.

The next layer was wetter and heavier. The digging slowed. I was about a foot down and getting dirtier.

I reached a thick root, maybe two inches around, running underneath the path. I hacked at it with my toy shovel, but barely dented it. Working my fingers around the root, I displaced the muddy sand from behind it. I grabbed ahold of the root but didn't have enough leverage to break it. I worked around it, pulling up more wet sand and dirt.

A pool of brown water filled the bottom of the hole, and my hands were freezing. Then my hand brushed against something. It felt smooth, like a sandwich bag.

I took the shovel and stabbed at the root over and over, chipping away at it. It helped. I grabbed more of whatever the thing was, and I worked it back and forth, side to side, trying to loosen it. It still wouldn't budge.

I got down on my stomach and reached my arm over the path and down into the hole. I finally got what felt like a solid grip, and pulled hard.

It was free. I had it in my hand. But I didn't pull it out of the hole. I just lay there, face down on the path, holding it. It was cube-shaped and maybe four by four inches. I could feel the ziplock edge of a plastic kitchen storage bag.

I rolled on to my back and looked up at the tree. I remembered it full and green in the summer. In the fall, Alyssa and I would dance around it while its leaves fell. I knew that pulling that thing out of its hiding place could mean something amazing for me and my family. And maybe people we would never even know. Or it could mean more trouble. More chases. I thought about reburying it, just sticking it deep back into the hole and packing it tight with sand so no one would ever find it.

But it was too late. Even knowing where that thing was left me in a dangerous situation: I knew *something*. And besides, I wasn't about to ignore what could be my dad's last message.

Mr. Hooper would be back any minute. I used the shovel and my good foot to push sand back into the hole. I tossed some tanbark and pine needles on top.

The sand had fewer pine needles near the merry-go-round. I used the shovel to clear a flat square space in the sand. I gathered some tanbark and used it to spell out a message in large capital letters. I left the shovel sticking out of the sand.

Mr. Hooper still wasn't here. I walked to the pay phone. From there, I would be able to see him pull up. I put in two quarters and dialed.

"Green Cab Company, can I help you?"

"I need a cab at Morris Park as soon as possible," I said. "I'll be near the basketball courts."

Maybe Mr. Hooper knew I wouldn't be there when he returned. I don't know. I do know that the Tank wouldn't stop until he found me. And if I was with my family, and you and Mr. Hooper, then I would be putting all of you at risk, not just myself. I couldn't do that to my brother and sister. I loved them too much.

I waited. My cab came. I got in.

"Where to, sport?" the driver asked.

"The bus station, downtown."

As we pulled away from the curb, something made me turn around. Through the back window, I could see the silhouette of a figure standing at the playground. I hoped it was Mr. Hooper. I hoped he saw my message in the sand:

I'M OK. GO.
JUSTIN.

CHAPTER 16:
The Road

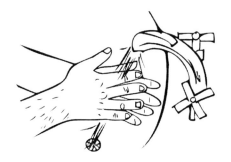

Downtown was busy. The sidewalks were packed with people. Traffic was backed up at stoplights. I had a sick feeling that the Tank was near. I dodged through the crowd and pushed open the glass doors to the bus station.

It was dark and quiet. My eyes adjusted. Everything was black and grey and brown. Vending machines leaned against one wall. Bus posters displayed that stupid slogan, "Let Us Take You There."

Behind the counter, a heavy-set woman in a grey uniform was sitting in front of a computer screen, reading a newspaper. She smiled at me and raised her eyebrows like she was asking, "Can I help you?" I nodded toward the restroom and kept walking, my footsteps echoing against the floor.

Just inside the bathroom, I nearly collided with a kid my height. His hair was messed up. His pants were dirty, and he carried a beat-up plastic bag. My first thought was that he was one of the younger homeless guys that camped out under the bridges and had come to the bus station to wash up and get warm. It took a second to realize that I was looking at myself in a full-length mirror.

I cleaned up as best as I could, washing my face, running my fingers through my hair, dusting off my pants. I checked the mirror again. I looked like a homeless kid that just used the bathroom.

I went to the pay phone. I couldn't remember what name Mr. Hooper had told me. Then it came to me: *South Bay Psychiatric Services.* I found the number in the phone book, stuck in a couple of quarters, and dialed.

"South Bay Psychiatric, can I help you?" Strong accent. Vietnamese, I guessed.

"I would like to talk to one of your patients, please," I said.

"Well, we have a confidentiality policy here," she said. "I can't even tell you if the person you want to speak to is a patient. All I can do is take a message. You tell me the name of the person, and give me your name and phone number. That's all I can do for you, OK?"

"Look, I understand that you have rules, but this is very important. I really need to talk to her. Her name is Desiree Tyme. I guess I'm asking you to bend the rules just this once."

"Ma'am, I'm sorry, but —"

"I'm a boy," I said.

"Oh, I'm sorry, sir —"

"Can you at least make a general announcement that I'm on the phone, so that the patients might hear it? Maybe she'll respond. *Please.* She'll want to know I'm calling."

It was quiet for a moment. I didn't know if that was good or bad.

"Sir, I'm *not* supposed to do this. Stay on the line." I heard a click on her end. I waited.

"Hello?"

The voice was unfamiliar — scratchy and soft. But I knew who it was. I didn't know how to feel or what to think or even what to say. It was like I was talking to my mom for the first time.

"Mom?"

"Justin, where are you?" Her words were slurred.

"I'm safe, I'm OK," I said. "So are Alyssa and Junior. They're with the Hoopers. Mr. Hooper found me."

"Oh, I remember now. Wait, but what..." Her voice trailed off.

"Mom, you didn't tell me about dad and his work. And Frank. Why?"

"Justin, you have to believe me," she said, slowly. "I wanted to, but I couldn't. Frank told me that he would — "

There was a loud crack on the line. It sounded like the phone hitting the floor.

"Boy, where are you?"

It was him. He was there with her. Of course. My heart was pounding. I felt the same adrenaline rush as when I ran from the cops.

Then something I had never experienced began to well up in me. I can only describe it as one half total calm and one half absolute rage. From inside the chaos of what my life had become, I finally knew who I was.

"Never mind where I am. I have what you want, you son-of-a-bitch. It's right here in my hands. I found it. Do you hear me? I have what you want!"

Silence. Then:

"I'm listening."

"Good. Then hear this: If you do anything to my family, I swear, you'll *never* see what I have. You got that? *Never.* Don't look for me. We'll be in touch."

I slammed the receiver down.

"Justin."

I turned around. It was Mr. Dave, standing there in his leather chaps and motorcycle jacket, holding his helmet.

"Mr. Dave, what are you doing here?" I asked. "How did you know where I was?"

"Listen," he said, "we need to talk." His gravely voice was almost a whisper. Something was wrong.

We sat. Mr. Dave held his helmet between his knees and looked down at the floor. I had never seen him in any mood but happy. The power I felt on the phone evaporated into the dark of the bus station.

"What's going on?" I asked.

"Justin, have you noticed all the help I've given you lately?"

"You mean the hundred bucks?" I answered. "I don't know what to say, except— thanks. A lot. I will definitely get it back to you as soon as I can, I promise."

"There was that," he said. "And the ride home after you turned your ankle. And the escape from the car. And the apartment."

Mr. Dave looked at me like I was supposed to figure something out. But I hadn't yet.

Then, I did. But I didn't want to believe it. I couldn't believe it.

"Are you saying that you know him?"

He nodded a 'yes'.

"You're — working with him?"

He nodded 'no'.

"Working for him?"

He dropped his head. Yes.

Time stood still. More people were at the station, buying tickets, checking luggage. A baby's cry echoed.

"Do you remember the picture of my son?" Mr. Dave asked.

"Yes," I said.

"I know you took the article from my shed."

"I'm sorry."

"It's OK," he said. "Did you read it?"

"Yes."

"Then you must know how desperate I was for money to get help for DeShawn."

"I only know what I read," I told him. "There was a fundraiser."

"That's right— and it didn't raise squat," he said. "I don't mean to sound unappreciative. It was incredible, how everyone rallied around DeShawn. But you have to understand how sick he was by then. He stayed home, in bed. His hair was falling out. He had lost so much weight that you could see the bones through his skin. And the chemo, the radiation treatment, wasn't helping. The doctors told me that his chances were basically zero. But I wasn't going to give up."

"Then I heard about this radical treatment that had worked for a kid back in Boston. I contacted the doctor. He told me that he was willing to help DeShawn, but that it would cost me. And I was already buried in debt from unpaid hospital bills."

"I was at Ben Harrison one day when a man showed up and asked to see me. You were in the third grade. We met in my office. He told me that he was aware of DeShawn's health problems, and that he could help. He said that he could take care of our money problems, if I was willing to help him in return."

"I was in shock," Mr. Dave said, shaking his head. "I mean, all of a sudden there was this guy sitting across from me who could help me give DeShawn a chance to *live*."

"What did he want from you?" I asked.

"The pass phrase to C-Metal."

"The pass phrase to —?"

"Justin, you don't have to pretend," he said. "I followed you again today. I saw you get in Darren Hooper's car and meet with your brother and sister. The trip to the park. I know you found what you were looking for."

My brain paused while I waited for what I would feel.

"You mean all the times I visited you in your office, all the talking and the advice and the donuts, that was just a lie?" I asked, my voice growing louder. "The whole time, you were just spying on me?" I wrapped the plastic bag around my wrist.

"Justin, no," he said. "Look, I admit that, at first, spending time with you was just something that Frank suggested. Get to know you, pick your brain— maybe you'd mention something about your dad, something he did or said that could help me find that pass phrase. Frank figured that Danny probably left you the phrase without you even knowing."

"But, as time went on, things started to change. I began to feel closer to you. Protective, even. As Deshawn got sicker, I felt like— well, I could see some of the energy of his life...in you." He stood up.

"But that's all in the past," he said, looking down at me. "Frank gave me the money for DeShawn's treatment. I promised to get him the pass phrase," he said. "And, even though Deshawn is dead now, I have to keep my promise."

"What are you going to do?" I asked.

"I'm going to wash my hands," he said.

"What?"

"I'm going into the bathroom to wash my hands," he said. "I like to do a thorough job. Wash all the oil off my fingers from the bike. It should take me at least ten minutes, maybe fifteen. If you're still here when I get back, I will keep my promise to Frank."

"And if I'm not?"

"Then I guess I can't keep my promise. And I'll deal with the consequences. Goodbye, little buddy."

Mr. Dave walked toward the bathroom. At the door, he turned and looked at me. He was smiling. It was the smile I remembered. The one I want to remember. He gave me a thumbs-up. Then he was gone.

CHAPTER 17:
The Ticket

I walked up to the counter. The lady put her newspaper down.

"Can I help you?"

"I need a one-way ticket."

"Traveling alone today?" She began typing on the keyboard.

"Yes."

"Destination?"

Epilogue

It's been dark a long time. I've been on the road, I don't know how long, going somewhere. The seat next to mine is empty. My reflection stares back at me from the big black window. It has to be morning soon.

I don't know why I'm still writing to you in the journal. You'll probably never read it. Maybe I'm still writing because it feels like the last connection to my old life.

I'm sorry you and Mr. Hooper had to leave to make sure my brother and sister were safe, but if it had to be someone, I'm glad it was you. I don't worry about them as much because I know they're with you.

Alyssa likes a snack after school, and she needs help with her times tables. Frank, Jr. loves to watch Ronny Rectangle in the morning. Please tell them that I think of them every day and that I love them very much. And that I will come back.

Where is Danny Tyme?

Follow Justin's journey in Book Two of the
Search a Darker Sky series,
"The Oregon Story"

About the Author

As a kid, Devik Schreiner had a bad haircut and wore his pants too short. He enjoyed reading almanacs, science fiction, and the backs of baseball cards. He plays the trumpet and piano, loves golf and the San Francisco Giants, and is known for balancing a pencil on his nose. Devik teaches middle school English and History in San Jose and lives in Los Gatos, California with his wife and twin girls. This is his first novel.

CPSIA information can be obtained at www.ICGtesting.com
Printed in the USA
270421BV00002B/9/P